M000087216

THE BOOK OF STORY RHYMES

DENA STEWART

MEDIA PRESS

The Book of Story Rhymes

Tales of Unpredictable People

and the Baggage they Carry

from the quirky mind of

Dena Stewart

© 2020 Dena Stewart. All rights reserved.

No part of this book may be reproduced in any form or by any electronic or mechanical means, including information storage and retrieval systems, without written permission from the author, except for the use of brief quotations in a book review.

This is a work of fiction. Names, characters, places and incidents are either the product of the author's imagination or are used fictitiously. Any resemblance to actual persons, living or dead, businesses, companies, events or locales is entirely coincidental.

Cover Artwork — "Letting go of Baggage"

18"x 24" painting by Dena Stewart

ISBN: 978-1-955468-02-2 (Hardcover edition)

ISBN: 978-1-955468-03-9 (Paperback edition)

ISBN: 978-1-955468-04-6 (Ebook edition)

Published by: IQ Media Press

CONTENTS

OTHER BOOKS BY DENA STEWART:

"Inner Peace ... It Isn't Out There!" a memoire

"Miami off the Page" anthology, Women Writers Group of
South Beach *"Transitions"* anthology, Women Writers Group of
South Beach

Website Links

ALIVEONSOUTHBEACH.COM

DENA STEWART ART

COMMUNITY ART

(Center for Folk and Community Art)

ALIVE ON SOUTH BEACH VIDEOS

This book is dedicated to Stewart Stewart,
my wonderful husband, my love.

His philosophy is inspirational —
"Always aspire to ten cuts above!"

Stewart Stewart website: aliveonsouthbeach.com

ACKNOWLEDGMENTS

I'd like to thank my editors
whose words are very clever.
Their input and their patience
were the keys to this endeavor.

THANK YOU

Alice Dressler –
checked grammar and spelling,
with tips to help make these stories compelling.

June Dressler –
made sure that each rhyme had a flow,
and shared thoughts on making some characters grow.

Marilyn L. Cohen –
saw when a passage was tense
and advised other words to increase its suspense.

Pamela Mayer –
knew when to laugh and when to be teary
so that no story turned out to be dreary.

Irene Sperber –
endowed welcoming praise,
as well as her wit to help tighten a phrase.

Women Writers Group of South Beach –
gave their honest review,
commending what worked, stating what to redo.

Stewart Stewart –
listened closely to what each rhyme said,
and offered ideas to move the message ahead.

Linda Winters –
was a reader, a fresh eye that was needed.
Her view caught the phrases that were added or deleted.

Ruth DiTucci –
"As I read these tales, I heard musical notes.
They could be lyrics for ballads," were her supportive quotes.

PROLOGUE

While riding public transit
I studied all the faces
of strangers going somewhere
and envisioned to what places.

I'd overhear them talking
and without being too rude
would listen quite intently,
never to intrude.

I'd guess from their expressions
if they were distressed,
then give them my reality
based on the way they dressed.

Waiting on a standing line
or walking on the street
inspired me to think about
folks I'd never meet.

This book's a compilation
of fictitious observations.
A mix of desperation
and mindful aspirations.

There may be hints of humor
or a negative summation,
with fast-paced, rhyming tales with twists
to blow your expectation!

WHO AM I?

Colin was told he was lucky
to have such a great mom and dad.
If not for Jenny and Peter,
most likely, his life would be sad.

Jenny and Peter were childless
until a newborn was found
wrapped in a colorful blanket
on a bench in the nearby playground.

They took him home and fed him,
then placed him on their bed.
They were set to give him up
but adopted him, instead.

Colin's complexion was swarthy,
Jenny and Peter's was fair.
Their eyes were blue, Colin's were brown.
And Colin had black wavy hair.

Jenny and Peter raised Colin
with love, as if he were their own.
They gave him a home and safety,
yet he was calamity prone.

Throughout high school and college
Colin questioned his roots.
He wanted to know where he came from
and ended up causing disputes.

Whenever he brought up the subject,
Jenny had no information.
So, rather than seek validation,
he tried to avoid aggravation.

Colin trained as a mechanic.
He was very adept with his hands.
His forte was fixing expensive cars
and meeting rich clients' demands.

This day, a Bentley was brought in.
Its owner appeared to be manic.
When Colin told her the engine was dead,
her eyes displayed absolute panic.

She took out a small, loaded pistol
and aimed it at Colin's broad chest.
With no warning to duck or find cover,
the bullets passed through his tool vest.

Just at that moment, a cop car passed by,
the officers heard the first shot.
Colin was rushed to the hospital.
She was detained on the spot.

A slug had lodged in his kidney.
No option but organ removal
and lengthy months of dialysis,
given with doctors' approval.

He really required a transplant,
but there was a risk of infection.
Unless the donor had blood just like his
the kidney would face sure rejection.

Peter and Jenny's blood didn't match.
Colin's, it turned out, was rare.
If a good donor was not found in time
his health would be beyond repair.

They advertised in the newspapers
for both blood and kidney donors.
But what was presented couldn't be used
despite strong and healthy owners.

Then, when Colin was very near death,
a woman who seemed rather tipsy
came to the hospital to donate blood.
She was a Romany gypsy.

The nurses said no without testing.
But each day that passed, he got worse.
When the gypsy returned with her offer,
this time they did a reverse.

Her blood was a good match with Colin's.
They were prepped for the operation.
The surgery went very smoothly —
the kidney showed cooperation!

When Colin was fully recovered,
on his list was to thank all concerned.
Number one was to seek out the gypsy,
whose whereabouts nobody learned.

She skipped out before being discharged,
and the name she had given was wrong.
But Colin continued doing his search
and followed each lead that seemed strong.

He located her in her parlor
gazing into a big crystal ball.
She looked up and said with a smile,
"I knew that one day you would call."

She studied his palm and recited,
"I see you want facts from your past,
though your parents gave you a good life
with devotion and care meant to last."

"I know that," was Colin's sharp answer.
"I'm grateful for all that they've done.
But I want to know why my birth mom
would abandon her infant, her son."

The gypsy paused for a moment
as she looked into Colin's bright eyes.
She cried as she answered his question.
"I will clear any wrong, you surmise."

"She did so to give you a future,
one with a chance to succeed.
Her sacrifice was meant to save you.
In essence, she did a good deed."

"So go give your parents a hug and a kiss
with the knowledge that you've met no other
than the woman who loved you enough to let go.
Be free, my son. *I'm* your birth mother."

THE REFERENCE LETTER

Nora was from rural Belfast.
Her dad was a mean drop-down drunk.
Her mother was sick and unstable.
Her brother, the local street punk.

Growing up, Nora had struggles.
Yet, she pursued an education.
She studied all aspects of service
and chose nursing as her vocation.

A newsreel about small town USA
with a clinic, got her inspired
to work hard and save all her money.
Then flee to the Land she desired.

Without introductory letters,
a hospital Nora admired
wouldn't accept her credentials
until one of their nurses retired.

Nora was given most of the tasks
that all other nurses deplore.
To tend to the sickest and dying,
as well as the hungry and poor.

As the newcomer to this small town,
to gain trust, and avoid all suspicion,
Nora signed up for volunteer work
at the regional Protestant Mission.

The congregants weren't accepting.
They labeled Nora *"capricious."*
Mocking her accent and lilting tone,
they spread gossip that bordered on vicious.

Nora was prone to depression
and fought hard to cope with her funk.
But sometimes her darkness would last
and, in pain, Nora imbibed and got drunk.

Though never when she was on duty.
She wouldn't let anyone see
her genetic predisposition.
She made sure to drink discreetly.

Yet one of the men in the Mission
saw Nora when not quite herself.
She had just downed what was left of the Rum
stored on the rectory's shelf.

With aggression and animal hunger,
he committed the wickedest rape.
He left her defenseless and wounded,
her spirit bound with broken tape.

The minister found Nora crying,
hysterical with fearful rage.
Instead of compassion and kindness,
he glared and went on a rampage.

He said, "You're no longer welcome
to join in and pray at my Mission.
Your volunteer service is worthless
because of your drunken condition."

He alerted the clinic she worked at.
With no recourse, Nora was fired.
She ran from this town to the city,
degraded, embarrassed, and tired.

In a metropolitan setting,
Nora searched for a job as a nurse.
But beset with negative references
her problems just seemed to get worse.

With not enough saved for her future,
Nora was out on the street.
Until by chance she noticed a sign,
"Here's Where Twelve Step Members Meet."

She went to the next AA meeting.
The members all grasped Nora's plight.
With their encouraging guidance,
she got back her spunk and her fight.

This time, when Nora applied for a job
she was welcomed and told not to worry.
The referral agency knew of a place
where they needed a nurse in a hurry.

"This rich lady, Anne, is eighty years old,
and often goes into a trance.
When she's alert, she's demanding,"
Nora was warned in advance.

So Nora was shocked when she met Anne.
This woman did not look her age.
Attired in ballgown and makeup,
she was set for bright lights and the stage.

As a Shakespearean actress,
Anne yearned to hear loud applause.
She complained that the nurse before Nora
was mean and brought up all her flaws.

Her barrister husband who died years before
made sure to leave her quite wealthy.
Affording the best care that money can buy,
Anne insisted she was very healthy.

She claimed to still have all her senses
and wasn't confused, like they said.
She just liked to play and have parties,
not waste her time lounging in bed.

The two hit it off within minutes.
They realized they needed each other.
Nora would give Anne the praise she desired,
and to Nora, Anne was like a mother.

Anne flourished for another decade,
Nora always by her side.
Their friendship was honest and caring,
restoring all of Nora's pride.

And when it was time for her to move on,
Nora had her reference letter.
Lady Anne happily lived ten more years.
Nora made her life so much better!

ROAD TO INNER PEACE

"Jenna is so fortunate,"
her aunts all said out loud.
"Her mother gives her everything.
Pray Jenna makes her proud."

Her mom came from a family
who practiced strict religion.
Choices weren't left to chance.
"Laws made the right decision."

Every time she broke a rule
her truth became inflated.
And when caught in a falsehood
she was critically berated.

As the middle child of ten,
her mom begged for attention.
But baby Jenna needed hers.
That led to mom's dissension.

Jenna's dad worked long hours,
frequently at night.
He didn't see when Jenna's mom
ignored her, out of spite.

During adolescence,
her mother criticized,
using words said with contempt.
Jenna felt ostracized.

When Jenna reached her middle teens
she reeked of apprehension.
Jenna's folks fought constantly,
and Jenna bore the tension.

Confiding in her thoughtless aunts,
Jenna bared her pain.
Their response was typically,
"Why is it you complain?"

"Your mother gives you everything,"
her mom's siblings defended.
"She goes without so you can have.
Be glad," they recommended.

Jenna worked her way through school.
She took required courses.
Her long-term goal was to be head
of corporate resources.

She taught office management
after graduation.
Then moved on to editing
to earn accreditation.

Still at home with mom and dad,
Jenna planned to move.
But first she must be married
for her parents to approve.

Jenna dated many guys.
A few steady relations.
When each ended, to bounce back,
Jenna took vacations.

With money saved, she traveled
to cities far and wide.
A respite from her family,
to restore her lost pride.

Then her best friend Maddy
arranged for a blind date.
Six months later Mike called.
He was worth the wait.

Mike worked as a publicist.
His clients were prestigious.
Jenna liked the glamour, and —
Mike was not religious.

Mike asked her to live with him.
For Jenna, a hard sell.
She wanted her mom's blessing.
Mom said, "Go to Hell!"

Her mother's disapproval
plagued Jenna all her life.
She hoped she'd find contentment
when she became Mike's wife.

But after they were married,
Jenna felt unchanged.
She realized she might need to have
her values rearranged.

So she and Mike took a long trip
to see what they would find.
They both learned they were looking for
freedom and peace of mind.

The trick was how to find it.
At this point neither knew.
It still seemed quite elusive,
from Jenna's point of view.

When they returned they did their best
to deal with their frustration.
Jenna landed a good job
in a large corporation.

Jenna thought this was the road
to bring her happiness —
her only way to please her mom
and be mistreated less.

But Jenna's mom kept nagging her
to have a child and quit.
Though stating quite emphatically,
"I will not babysit."

She didn't care that Jenna's mental health
had now regressed.
Her emphasis was on herself
and how her daughter dressed.

Jenna had her meltdown
on the day that she was fired.
Everything that could, went wrong.
Her zest for life expired.

Jenna saw a therapist
out of desperation.
"Your mother is the problem,"
was the Shrink's evaluation.

He said that Jenna's mother
had a need to see her fail.
"Your mother wants total control,
and all that would entail."

When Jenna swallowed the hard truth,
she faced her inner dread.
She left her family and friends.
With Mike, she forged ahead.

It didn't happen overnight
but Jenna's wounds did heal.
And as her resolve strengthened
she found that she could feel.

To fill her empty hours
she painted, first for fun.
Mike, too, became a painter.
Their quest had now begun.

As artists, she and Mike moved
from New York to trendy South Beach.
There, they blossomed rapidly
and used their art for outreach.

Jenna started writing
short stories, at the start.
Through characters she could reveal
the secrets in her heart.

After twenty years estranged,
she and mom conversed.
Jenna voiced her anguish.
Mom said, "Sorry," as rehearsed.

Soul-searching helped her clarify
and understand her past.
"Inner Peace, it's not out there,"
was what she learned, at last.

Jenna wrote a memoire
based on what she could deduce
were the reasons for her mom's
emotional abuse.

Jenna's book was published.
It surpassed her expectation.
"To Mom, who gave me everything,"
read Jenna's dedication.

TOO LITTLE — TOO LATE

Martha was the eldest
in a family of eight.
At seventeen she married Joe —
her period was late.

She gave birth to daughter Rose
eight months from when they wed.
Less than two years later,
Martha birthed a son named Ted.

Joe was a fair provider,
though Martha gave no raves.
She pushed him to work harder
when Joe would not make waves.

Martha was judgmental
and stubborn as a mule.
Embarrassed, she would cover up
she hadn't finished school.

Martha thrived on gossip.
Her input, rarely nice.
She loved to snoop and meddle
and give others her advice.

"Life has been so good to me,"
Martha would loudly boast,
making sure her words were heard
by those who suffered most.

She hated signs of weakness.
"One must always be strong."
But Martha lost her balance
whenever things went wrong.

When Martha was unhappy
she grabbed attention quickly.
She either threw a tantrum
or managed to look sickly.

Her daughter Rose got married
when World War II broke out.
Her husband, Bill, stayed stateside.
Her brother had less clout.

Ted was sent to England
where great misfortune struck.
They said he was killed instantly.
"Run over by a truck."

A tragedy unthinkable,
Ted's death left a huge scar.
Martha milked her misery
to make herself a star.

Martha started blacking out,
a side effect of grief.
The doctors said the spells would last,
some long, and sometimes brief.

This was the beginning
of a whole series of ills.
Surgery included,
as well as many pills.

Rose convinced her parents
that they should not live alone.
Her dad, too, had some ailments,
and was quite disaster prone.

Rose and Bill had sympathy
and an extra room.
Her parents came to live with them.
Now, gloom had turned to doom.

When Rose's friends came over
Martha played the boss.
Courtesy was given
to distract her from her loss.

But Rose was stripped of privacy
with Martha now around.
Martha tried to get involved
each time Rose made a sound.

When Joe, her dad, passed away,
Rose wanted back her space.
She helped Martha relocate
to a nearby place.

Martha went to visit Rose
at least three times a week.
And Martha had some neighbors
with whom to shop and speak.

After a while Martha was back
to her old active ways.
She played canasta every night
and mahjong during the days.

Rose was the one who got the brunt
of Martha's every ache.
What Martha needed, Rose would give,
and Martha sure did take.

Rose had worked hard all her life,
her dues were paid at last.
She now was ready to retire.
She and Bill had aged fast.

They bought a home in Florida
and made it quite explicit,
"Martha could come twice a year,
each time for a brief visit."

Martha was beside herself
with Rose so far away.
She wouldn't complain to her friends
who now kept her at bay.

At ninety, Martha still had wit,
aggressive as a hawk.
But a polyp on her throat
made it hard to talk.

Yet she called Rose twice each day
to tell her, "Life's not pretty."
She complained about her voice
and wallowed in self-pity.

One day Rose exploded.
She said she'd had enough.
Martha stunned by this response,
hung up in a huff.

When Rose didn't call right back,
Martha felt betrayed.
This was the very first time
that her daughter disobeyed.

Martha viewed Rose as her child
to whom she could tell all.
So after several weeks of silence,
Martha made the call.

She was set to forgive Rose.
For once, suck up her pride.
But Bill picked up the phone, not Rose.
"Rose had a stroke. She died!"

PATTERNS TO BREAK

Doreen met Tom in college
and with great anticipation
they were engaged, then married
soon after graduation.

They shared a common vision
and vowed, *"Until the end,*
we'll be there for each other
as would a true best friend."

When Tom went on to law school,
Doreen paid the bills.
Tom promised he would reimburse,
"One day, we'll have the frills."

Hired by a law firm
well known and quite impressive,
Tom was made Associate
for being so aggressive.

Tom won a major civil suit.
For that, a grand reward —
a million-dollar settlement,
and A.B.A. Award.

As quickly as his money came,
that's how the two were spending.
They fixed their house and bought a car,
the list was never ending.

What pioneered their vision
Tom met, as their intent.
But Doreen had no purpose,
which she started to resent.

So she went back to college
to earn a dual degree
in Family Dynamics
and Psychotherapy.

She started up a practice
for patients in distress.
She helped them see bad patterns
and persist under duress.

Then Tom did the unspeakable.
At a Firm retreat, he cheated.
Doreen found out. He swore to her,
"This tryst won't be repeated."

Not ready to give up on Tom,
to mend her saddened heart
Doreen thought a baby
would give them a new start.

Tom said he wasn't ready
to give his time and care.
He wanted kids to be a treasure
both of them would share.

Doreen stopped using birth control
without Tom's consultation.
Nine months later she gave birth.
Tom showed no jubilation.

Incensed by her deception,
Tom would drink and shout.
Now busy with her baby boy
Doreen froze Tom right out.

So Tom worked longer hours.
Doreen led healing sessions.
Hearing others speak their angst,
she forgave Tom's transgressions.

This time, Tom got so aroused
and enveloped in passion,
he didn't wear a condom
in his customary fashion.

So Doreen became pregnant,
and Tom had an affair.
She threatened to divorce him.
He said he didn't care.

Tom blamed Doreen for trickery
and baffling deception.
She agreed, then stated,
"You did not use contraception!"

He raged at her for mocking him,
belittling his choice.
She said that she was sorry
for castrating his voice.

Their divorce became final
when their baby girl was born.
Custody arrangements made,
both parents were forlorn.

Tom found a large apartment
a mile down the street.
Far enough for privacy
but close when they must meet.

Tom had the kids on weekends.
He said it was his pleasure
to see his daughter giggle,
and his son's growth, beyond measure.

Then Tom met Jill, and within months
the two became engaged.
Blinded by Jill's youthful poise,
he missed the times she raged.

Without proof, Doreen had perceived
Jill used the pain Tom carried
to access his large bank account.
Jill's reason to get married.

Until one Sunday, when brought back,
their son had a bruised arm.
Doreen accused Tom's *fiancé*
of doing her child harm.

Tom watched as Jill snarled with hate,
declaring Doreen, "Jealous!"
With head held high, Doreen replied,
"You're wrong. I'm super zealous."

Caught between the two, Tom said,
"I ran down to the store.
When I returned, our son cried that
his arm caught in the door."

So Doreen needed evidence
for action to be taken.
"Tom must see abuse, firsthand,
before he will awaken."

Tom's neighbor got what Doreen asked.
The woman was her client.
"I saw Tom's lady shove your son.
He looked sad and defiant."

She also said, Jill's froufrou dog
howled all day long.
She photographed its pile of poop
where it did not belong.

Words and pictures left no doubt
that Jill was quite unfit
to be trusted with his kids.
Tom made a swift exit.

He asked Doreen to "try again,"
all for their children's sake.
Tom promised to be true, this time.
"I've learned from my mistake."

Doreen said, "No" to Tom's return.
"Our pattern has to end.
But we'll be there for each other,
as would a true best friend."

IF YOU'RE IN IT

Gail bought her Lotto ticket
and stuck it in her purse.
She went on to the hospital
where she worked as a nurse.

Nursing had inspired Gail
when she was very young
and saw the care they gave her mom
when she punctured her lung.

Gail's father was a merchant.
His salary was meager.
Though giving to his family,
he was always eager.

He would do without a meal
if Gail needed new shoes.
His values were clear and concise.
He never had to choose.

Gail's manner was quite serious,
reticent, and shy.
She was the type of person
on whom others would rely.

Although she had a few good friends,
Gail rarely socialized.
It took a lot of effort
for her dream to be realized.

She didn't have a scholarship
to pay for nursing school.
So in between her classes
she worked in a steno pool.

It took Gail more than twice the time
to complete required training.
But when she got her nurse's cap,
she forgot years of complaining.

Gail was dedicated
and thrilled to reach her goal.
She was immersed in her career
with full body and soul.

The patients in the ward Gail worked
were very close to death.
The nurse on call would witness them
taking their final breath.

At other times, the nurses saw
the patients' will to live.
They realized that they were the ones
with so much more to give.

For Gail it was the greatest pleasure
when she would discover
that a patient had a chance
to totally recover.

Gail said that she was fulfilled
in her selfless profession,
but needed a hiatus
after a wretched session.

A patient she had cared for
succumbed and passed away.
Gail was affected by this loss,
much more than she would say.

Right at that time a friend of Gail's
was going on a cruise.
She asked Gail to come along.
Gail did not refuse.

Years before, a jaunt was scratched
when Gail's dad caught the flu.
This time Gail would take no chance.
Time off was overdue.

She made all the arrangements.
Another nurse would cover.
Gail dared to have rare daydreams
about a shipboard lover.

The day of her departure
Gail got an urgent call.
They said it wasn't dire
but her mom took a bad fall.

Gail put her fantasy on hold,
her mind now on her mother.
Prepared to lose her needed trip,
"One day I'll take some other."

Gail's mom was not hurt badly,
but she said she couldn't walk.
The accident had frightened her.
She needed Gail to talk.

Although she wasn't happy,
Gail hid her disappointment.
She helped her mom do exercise
and dressed her wounds with ointment.

Gail went straight back to her job.
Without her planned vacation,
she was jittery and anxious
with more pent-up frustration.

She spent most of her day on shift
except when time for lunch.
In the cafeteria,
she joined a noisy bunch.

Gail listened to the people talk
about the daily news.
Sharing items in the Post,
they argued different views.

She heard somebody mention
the latest Power Ball.
"They picked the lucky numbers.
Someone had won it all."

A doctor read the numbers off
joking all the while,
as others told how they would spend
the money in grand style.

Gail didn't pay attention
until she realized
that all the numbers that were called
were those she recognized.

Gail hadn't checked her ticket,
her day had been so rotten.
It still was somewhere in her purse,
buried and forgotten.

She quickly found her Lotto slip
to see if she heard right.
And when her numbers were reread,
she screamed with pure delight.

With ninety million dollars,
Gail felt no hesitation
to take a leave, go on that cruise,
and savor relaxation.

LIVING UP TO A LEGACY

Jerry was the son
of a New York City cop
who demanded Jerry be
untarnished and tip top.

The discipline applied at work
he used upon his son.
Whenever Jerry misbehaved,
his dad took out his gun.

As Jerry grew, most things he did
created a commotion.
While he was strictly punished,
his dad gained a promotion.

Dad's rank raised to detective.
Soon after, he made chief.
While everyone commended him,
all Jerry got was grief.

*"It's one thing when you're dealing with
your dad's superiority.
Another when your dad is named
the highest of authority."*

Soon after Jerry turned eighteen
he was told to reform.
"Join the Navy!" his dad said,
demanding he conform.

When enlisted, Jerry fronted
shipmates in his section.
In combat, it was Jerry who
prevented their defection.

Back home, Jerry was compelled
to take risks, all were temptation.
Only when conniving
did he have the "spark" sensation.

Jerry played the horses.
He high-rolled to get rich.
But the more that Jerry gambled,
the deeper was his ditch.

Jerry swore all this would change.
"I will be a winner, yet!"
Then he went to the casino
and lost another bet.

While Jerry had more failures,
his father earned more power.
In his dad's huge shadow
Jerry wilted as he'd cower.

With no end to his setbacks,
Jerry donned a wig and mask.
Armed with a toy pistol,
he set upon his task.

He slipped the Bank clerk a curt note.
It said, "I won't do harm.
Just hand me all the cash you have.
And don't press the alarm."

When Jerry planned this Bank heist
he knew a silent bell
was hooked up to a help line.
SWAT came like bats from Hell.

With loaded ammunition
they gunned the robber down.
When they removed his costume
they recognized the *clown.*

"Tell my dad, I'm sorry!"
Jerry said, with his last breath.
"Deliberate Suicide by Cop,"
was Jerry's cause of death.

"I seemed to miss all of the signs
that my son was defective,"
his father said, when interviewed
as New York's Chief Detective.

BALLROOM DANCER

Rita starts each day by asking,
"So what's new with you?"
as though she's really interested
in everything we do.

And when we tell her, "Nothing much,"
she probes a little more.
She asks if we bought anything
in the department store.

When we don't answer her at length,
she then goes on to say,
"I think that you're unhappy.
Why do you feel that way?"

If we exclaim that we are fine,
she asks why we're evasive.
She says she wants to be our friend,
but we find her abrasive.

She pries into our home life
claiming she's just curious.
Her questions are so personal
she often makes us furious.

When we try to ignore her,
she looks like she might cry.
The details of her private life
she's anxious to supply.

But her life is so boring.
Her every move controlled
by her relentless mother
who's persnickety and old.

Rita still lives with her mom,
although she's forty-five.
"I will continue doing so
as long as mom's alive."

She's worked for the same boss for years
and claims he's very rude.
But when asked why she doesn't quit,
she justifies his mood.

Rita talks about her friends.
She shares their tales in detail.
Boasting for them when they win,
unfriending them when they fail.

Rita's done some traveling,
mostly with group tours.
She then tells stories only of
the places she abhors.

Once, when she complained to us
how dull her life turned out,
"Why don't you lighten up, have fun,"
to Rita we dared shout.

We asked her what she'd want to do
given a second chance.
To our surprise she told us that
she'd love to learn to dance.

She said when young she tried ballet,
but wasn't any good.
"Ballroom dancing lessons
I would take now, if I could."

We questioned what was stopping her.
"My mother is," she stated.
"My mom cannot be left alone
when she's ill and sedated."

We made a few suggestions.
Rita said okay
to taking some dance classes.
"With my mom, a friend will stay."

Rita, at first, was nervous.
This type of action, new.
But once she took her first dance step
she had a broader view.

She then made sure three times a week
to have a neighbor in
to visit with her mom so she'd
be free to twirl and spin.

She made up for her absences
by showing her devotion.
Her mother laughed when Rita
demonstrated each dance motion.

Rita's life had purpose now.
Dancing, her release
from mundane incidentals.
And her self-worth did increase.

Shortly, Rita made new friends
and even started dating.
Rita's conversations now
were far more stimulating.

Rita's disposition changed.
She basked in her new life.
She quit her job when asked to be
her dance instructor's wife.

Her mother's main unspoken fear,
"What will become of me?"
diminished when they found a house
that's big enough for three.

Now Rita celebrates the date
she got her second chance.
We just received our invitation
to her Wedding Dance.

THE LENNY SAGA

His mom had postpartum depression
and cried that she was deprived
of quiet and a good night sleep.
But baby Lenny still thrived.

His smiling disposition
and easy attitude
softened frenzied moments
and brightened up her mood.

He had an older sister
and then, a younger brother.
Sandwiched in between the two,
he linked them to each other.

Their dad, who worked long hours,
played no active role
in raising his three children.
"Providing," was his goal.

From elementary through high school
Lenny passed each test
without too many questions
so that he was not a pest.

He grew to be quite handsome,
six feet tall and thin.
Competitive in sports and games,
Benny played to win.

He enrolled in college
for a path to a career.
He took assorted courses,
then dropped out within a year.

Lenny had a lot of friends.
He was generous and nice.
His loyalty caused them to say,
"Your big heart is your vice."

At twenty-one, he got engaged.
The girl was free with hugs.
She broke it off before they wed,
then overdosed on drugs.

Without a clear-cut roadmap
Lenny had no plan.
He quit his part-time sales job
and with cash saved, bought a van.

He left New York and went out west
and settled in L.A.
Two years later he returned,
burned out from too much play.

Lenny joined his brother
in his brother's business deal.
Lenny sold his gem designs
and boosted their appeal.

But at the height of their success
their dad had a bad ailment.
Lenny sacrificed his time
to stop their mom's derailment.

Then Lenny fell in love again.
She urged, "Go back to school.
We'll marry when you graduate."
That was her iron rule.

He majored in psychology
for a Masters' degree.
Then his love was in a crash
and was killed instantly.

Lenny had more options now
that he had good credentials.
He turned down offers of big bucks,
preferring bare essentials.

He got work in a hospital
to treat mental disease.
He made light of intensity
to keep patients at ease.

Secure in his profession,
when his mom became demented,
Lenny thought to hire an aide.
His siblings both consented.

Lenny had an apartment,
but was on Mom's co-op Deed,
giving him rights to all that she owned
so her welfare was guaranteed.

Recommended by a friend,
Leah became Mom's caregiver.
She was the only one interviewed.
Lenny hoped that she could deliver.

Leah was from Sochi, Russia.
She convinced Lenny he picked a winner.
In her mid-thirties, attractive and neat,
when he visited, she served him dinner.

She coyly appealed to his sympathy
with a story that her life was hard.
"My dream is to be an American
with an authentic U.S. Green Card."

Lenny had a noble idea
to skip years of INS rancor.
"Why don't we become husband and wife?
I'll be your American anchor."

Relationships hadn't worked out for him.
Both of his true loves had died.
Middle aged now, with no prospects,
he thought this a favor, with pride.

Leah jumped at his offer
and willingly signed a release.
A notarized prenup relinquishing all,
spelling out when their union would cease:

"Once Leah's a tax-paying National,
and expulsion cannot be enforced,
with no strings attached, no financial gain,
this couple will then get divorced."

Lenny told only his siblings.
Their reactions were as he predicted,
"Her motives are selfish and yours are to please.
Be careful or you'll be convicted."

In marriage, they were not together.
But on paper, both used Mom's address.
Leah was on Lenny's Medical plan.
He claimed friendship, not under duress.

For two years, Leah lived with his mom.
Then Mom fell. This gave all a scare.
Leah went on to a job somewhere else,
and Mom sent to Hospice, for care.

When his mom died, he fixed up her co-op,
moved in, and lived there alone.
Lenny's connection to Leah
was through text message or telephone.

All Leah's mail was forwarded.
There was rarely a need for a meeting.
Lenny was waiting for the right time
for their fraud to no longer be cheating.

But, when citizenship was granted,
Leah stated, with great acrimony,
"As your legal wife, if we were to divorce,
I expect to be paid alimony."

At sixty-five, Lenny retired.
Leah wanted some pay from his pension
and demanded she keep his Insurance.
He agreed, just to lower his tension.

Leah had never been part of his group.
His troubles, he didn't confide.
His friends nor his siblings asked questions,
to them Lenny never had lied.

Then, Lenny was late for their dinner,
"A trait not like Lenny, at all."
His brother became apprehensive
when he didn't respond to his call.

Two hours of off-and-on worry,
his brother went to his apartment.
Strewn on the floor were some documents
and an open bureau compartment.

Lenny was in his bedroom.
Fully dressed, flat on his back.
His face fully drained of color.
"DEAD!" from a huge heart attack.

Lenny's Will was with his papers.
He bequeathed to his sister and brother,
his possessions and Deed to the co-op,
as stipulated by their mother.

To Leah, his wife in name only,
who refused to give him back his ring,
as per their prenup agreement
he left "Love — and not one more thing!"

Lenny's epitaph was befitting:
"He was loyal, giving, and nice.
He never said "NO" or refused those in need.
His big heart was truly his vice."

THE FORCE BEHIND HER DRIVE

Earning lots of money
was the force behind her drive.
Although she rarely spent it,
it gave her cause to strive.

From infancy until age six,
in an Asian land,
Liling was raised by a "friend"
as her father planned.

In time for school, she was returned
to small town New York State.
Here, Liling lived with family.
But she could not relate.

With strangers now called
Mom and Dad, as well as a big sister,
Liling had to navigate
this real-world game of twister.

In school, Liling was ridiculed
for her foreign intonation,
making her self-conscious
of her mispronunciation.

Although her father gave her toys,
her mother was aloof.
Liling's statements were deemed lies
until backed up with proof.

Her sister was competitive,
where Liling was quite smart.
She recognized she must outdo
to be taken to heart.

Liling was imposing
with an overt need to please.
Every chance to show her worth
Liling jumped to seize.

The day Liling turned eighteen
she learned of the arrangement
for her to marry Dad's "friend's" son.
He agreed to their engagement.

This matchup came as quite a shock.
She had nowhere to run.
So Liling married JunJie.
Then birthed Bolin, their son.

Soon after, JunJie, a craftsman,
was in a head on crash.
Now, no longer fit to work,
to live, they needed cash.

"I'll get a job," Liling declared.
She had good skills to write.
Hired by a tabloid rag,
she covered sex and blight.

Then, JunJie, without warning,
filed for divorce.
Liling took young Bolin
and left with no remorse.

She moved back in with Mom and Dad.
Mom scoffed at her writing.
To Bolin, she was kinder,
but he saw internal fighting.

When Liling's father passed away,
Mom turned even meaner.
Liling's pal, Chang, rescued her.
His house was big and cleaner.

Chang, a truck mechanic,
liked having her around.
And Bolin gave him purpose.
He kept Chang duty-bound.

Chang urged Liling to find work
in a field that was new.
Liling, who was quick to learn,
went for the interview.

Hired by a big Tech firm
in the Internet's young stage,
she earned large sums of money
when dotcoms were the rage.

She bought Mom her own co-op.
For that, she hoped for praise.
Instead, Mom accused Liling
of falling for a craze.

Then Mom, while cooking, cut herself.
She needed a transfusion.
Liling went to donate blood,
but was deemed an intrusion.

That's when Liling learned the truth.
Her dad had an affair
with Mom's niece, Liling's cousin.
She was their child, their heir!

This cousin gave up all her rights
to Liling, with no meeting.
She was banned from the family —
"Prevent scandal from repeating."

This explained why Liling bore
Mom's cruel verbal beating.
Liling was a token of
her husband's faithless cheating.

Too much to process and accept
from this discovery,
Liling had a heart attack.
With luck, a full recovery.

To mend her wounded psyche,
and expose things she thought wrong,
Liling launched a website
to post views. Hers were quite strong.

She wanted mass approval.
Instead, she got pushback.
The consequence of animus —
a second heart attack.

Without any insurance
and a profound precondition,
Liling wed Ming, with a health plan.
He dragged her to perdition.

Ming, a gun shop owner,
became Manic Depressive.
And after many ups and downs
turned angry and aggressive.

With Bolin, she moved back with Chang,
platonic and rent free.
Chang bolstered her delusions.
When she vented, he'd agree.

As time continued, Bolin learned
hi-tech computer coding.
He researched cryptocurrency,
another field, exploding.

To help with Liling's quest for cash
and ease her fears and doubt,
Bolin told her, "Crypto Coins
is what it's all about."

In coins, Liling invested
to be grandiose and rich.
For this, Mom told her mockingly,
"You'll wind up in a ditch."

"One day I'll be a billionaire,
and you'll want my respect,"
Liling retorted angrily.
"Revenge, you can expect."

This was the thought on Liling's mind
that kept her right on track
to be in Forbes 400
as a leader of the pack.

She wanted satisfaction,
and to demonstrate her worth
to this woman she called Mom.
Although not hers through birth.

But when she cashed in all her coins
and had all this vast wealth,
Mom, who always put her down
had terminal ill health.

Then, Liling's nasty sister,
whom she hardly ever saw,
trash talked that she's "pathetic,"
a jab to Liling's craw.

This "punch" was her awakening.
*"My benevolence is not for sale.
Why waste my time and energy
on those who wished I'd fail."*

So when, at last, Mom passed away,
her angst was put aside.
Liling's classy tribute
was with self-respect and pride.

Acceptance of reality
helped clarify her drive.
*"My natural need for a mom's love
was what forced me to strive."*

With this in-depth awareness
Liling spent her massive wealth
on pleasure, friends and Bolin.
And, to maintain her good health!

THE STUTTERING SINGER

Quite simply, Sean was talented.
Articulate and smart,
okay at sports, and popular.
Off to a decent start.

He played a few string instruments,
and his singing voice was great.
"To be the lead in a rock band,"
Sean hoped would be his fate.

He formed a group with several friends.
They practiced when convenient.
Sean was way more disciplined
when they were stoned and lenient.

Sean had a little brother, Max.
For Max, Sean was the best.
He loved to listen to Sean sing.
Sean thought Max was a pest.

One day, when Sean needed his space,
his music didn't flow,
young Max was getting antsy.
Sean yelled at Max to go.

Dismissed by Sean who tuned him out
while strumming his guitar,
Max ran out into the street
and was hit by a car.

Sean heard the crash. He saw his brother
lying in the gutter.
Racked with guilt for what he'd done,
all Sean could do was sputter.

Sean lost all of his confidence.
Each time he tried to speak,
he stuttered very badly
and his once great voice would squeak.

Disgusted by the sounds he made,
Sean had much self-disdain.
"I can't perform. What's left for me?"
His dreams went down the drain.

Even after Max had healed
and was back up to speed,
Sean carried lots of heavy guilt
so he could not succeed.

Sean went to a speech therapist
who helped the best he could.
But Sean was not receptive
so his techniques did no good.

Sean, instead, wrote lyrics
and his songs were all big hits
for other Rock Band singers.
For Sean, it was the pits.

Sean spent most of his time alone
until one summer day
he went to a rock concert.
A lady came his way.

Faye wore exotic dresses
and she had a pretty smile.
She saw through Sean's impediment
and knew he was worthwhile.

Faye said, "I, too, once stammered,
my speech was not okay.
It cleared when I no longer cared
what others had to say."

Faye's attitude attracted Sean
and soon they started dating.
With Faye, Sean gained back his esteem
and stopped self-deprecating.

Faye helped Sean see how past events
had caused his speech affliction
and how it had become
a psychological addiction.

Sean had no valid reason
for his psyche to be marred.
His guilt was self-inflicted,
as his brother wasn't scarred.

Sean finally agreed to try
and overcome his fear.
Faye gave him her encouragement
which Sean knew was sincere.

Faye held her breath and waited,
afraid of what she'd hear
until Sean started singing,
at first low, but crystal clear.

When Sean was finished with his song,
not a sound did Faye dare utter.
So Sean repeated what he sang,
in words without a stutter.

The lyrics for the tune Sean wrote
told how Faye changed his life.
And in those written words he asked
if she would be his wife.

Of course, Faye said she'd marry him.
"I'd love to wear your ring."
Their wedding took place at a show
that Sean was booked to sing.

A MANAGER'S GREATEST GIFT

Frank was a talent manager.
His role was like playing a father
to his clients, all actors.
For them, business was a big bother.

Frank helped them set up auditions.
For that, he charged a fair price.
He used this fee to pay his rent,
and the actors got his sound advice.

Married and divorced three times,
Frank was a terrible mate.
But when he had a job to do
his efforts were all first rate.

At forty-eight Frank still had hopes
that his clients one day would gain fame.
But none of them had that rare quality
required in that talent game.

Then Ryan walked into his office.
He auditioned with a song and dance.
Ruggedly gaunt and charming,
Frank opted to give him a chance.

Frank said he would be in charge
of scheduling Ryan's appointments.
They signed a written agreement
to avoid all disappointments.

Ryan needed guidance,
and so a fair deal was struck.
Frank kept track of all callbacks,
and Ryan had lots of good luck.

Quite quickly Ryan got acting work
which led to bigger roles.
He fit the brooding misfit type.
Frank helped him reach his goals.

Ryan valued Frank's management,
mentoring, friendship, and aid.
From Ryan's sizable paychecks,
Frank's salary was amply paid.

And as Ryan's stardom grew,
he was exposed to more.
He met many casting agents
who launched new roads to explore.

And everywhere that Ryan went,
Frank trailed close behind
relishing what Ryan had.
Ryan didn't mind.

Just before he met Frank,
he verged on suicide.
It was Frank who pushed him off
his self-destructive ride.

So when those agents labeled Frank
a sponging parasite,
Ryan stood up for the man
who eased him from his plight.

Frank's words reassured him
when Ryan voiced defeat.
He'd say, "You'll win an Oscar,
so that my work is complete."

Soon, Ryan moved to Hollywood.
Frank chose to stay behind.
As Ryan built his fan base,
Frank's words stayed on his mind.

Frank joked that he would visit
when Ryan had the lead
in a big splash five-star movie.
Ryan laughingly agreed.

At first, he called Frank every week.
Then twenty years went by.
No longer were there catch-up calls,
and all contact went dry.

Ryan met an actress
who starred in TV shows.
They married and earned money
that took care of all their woes.

They had a son and daughter
and moved into a mansion
with tennis courts, a pool and gym,
and more land for expansion.

As characters became the norm,
Ryan played the part.
When nominated for the "Prize"
he took Frank's words to heart.

He placed a call to his old friend
to remind him of his joke
and invite Frank for that visit.
But was told Frank had a stroke.

"Frank was so debilitated,
he could barely walk.
His left side was immobile
and he didn't want to talk."

Ryan flew East to New York
to see what he could do
to give his old friend comfort.
Then he hired a building crew.

On his land he had erected
a lodge where Frank would stay.
Then red tape for a full-time nurse
caused Frank a move delay.

But Ryan made it happen
with no room for debate.
Within a month Frank made the trip
to where he'd relocate.

.The eve of the Academies,
Frank watched from his recliner.
When Ryan won the Oscar,
Frank said, "Nothing could be finer!"

That night, Ryan placed the Statue
next to Frank's bedside.
With tears of grace and gratitude,
Frank closed his eyes and died.

THE GIFT TO TWO BROTHERS

Don and Harry's mother
was small-town with big goals.
Sadly, she hooked up with Jake
who raked her over coals.

Jake, a sexy bad boy,
scammed and went to jail.
Pregnant with their first born, Don,
her money paid Jake's bail.

After their son Harry's birth,
Jake robbed a local bank.
He was locked up a second time.
To ease her angst, she drank.

With two young boys to care for
and sick of his abuse,
she kicked Jake out forever.
No need for an excuse.

When Don and Harry reached their teens,
she met another lout.
When her sons said they loathed him,
their mother threw them out.

Don, the elder, was eighteen
when he finished school.
Harry quit at age sixteen,
but was skilled with a tool.

Timothy, their uncle,
found them a place to stay.
They had a roof over their heads,
but needed work to pay.

As an actor, Timothy
was suave and debonair.
He introduced his nephews
to Jerome, a millionaire.

Jerome, his longtime lover,
had known pain of rejection.
Though Don and Harry both were straight,
they, too, suffered dejection.

As earnest as Jerome was,
Timothy was funny.
Both of them were generous
and slipped the brothers money.

Jerome, a known collector,
gave the boys antiques
to sell for him at the street fair,
set up every two weeks.

Jerome also had fine art
he bought and then exported.
Don or Harry drove his truck
when paintings were transported.

This night, Harry drove the van.
A cop thought he was drunk.
He was accused of robbery
when told to pop the trunk.

While placing him in handcuffs,
he spun Harry around.
Though Harry claimed his innocence,
he was pushed to the ground.

Harry was arrested and
forced to stay in jail
for an entire night and day.
Jerome posted his bail.

Timothy, their uncle,
paid for both boys' education.
Jerome said that he wouldn't miss
their college graduation.

The brothers studied very hard
and both got their degree.
Harry in mechanics,
Don in psychology.

At their commencement service,
they saw the vacant chair.
Timothy was all alone.
"Why wasn't Jerome there?"

Not to ruin Don and Harry's
rewarding event,
Timothy kept to himself
news he could not prevent.

With teary eyes, he told the boys
Jerome had passed away.
He had a sudden heart attack
early in the day.

But just before he closed his eyes,
right before he died,
he handed Timothy his Will
that said all he'd provide.

Don and Harry would inherit
his antique collection,
valued in the millions
upon close inspection.

Jerome bequeathed to Timothy
all else that he had saved,
with one major condition.
"He must do what he craved."

A true friend to the very end,
Jerome changed all their lives.
Timothy directed plays.
Both brothers met their wives.

A GREAT ESCAPE

Kim and Neil wed at nineteen.
Ben was born one year later.
Kim quit school to care for him,
Neil got a job as a waiter.

What started as a true romance
ended when they fought.
Neil would shove and smack her.
Kim was left distraught.

Divorce came when Kim had enough.
Neil paid no child support
nor any alimony.
Though, he worked in a swank resort.

With two years of college behind her,
Kim had few usable skills.
So she and Ben lived with her parents
who grudgingly paid all their bills.

Kim's father was a car salesman
who spent weekdays out on the road.
Her mother was a stenographer.
Kim bore the housekeeping load.

Ben, as a child, was allergy prone,
giving reason for Kim to be frightened.
With Ben in danger of choking or worse
Kim's anxiety level was heightened.

Neil came around when convenient.
He gave Ben food that made him sick.
When Ben had a toxic reaction,
Neil fled the scene very quick.

When Ben was placed in first grade,
Kim worked in a small retail store —
a menial job and low paycheck.
Her dream was to one day have more.

While stacking shelves in Men's Wear,
Jayson walked into the aisle.
He needed a shirt to go with his suit
and unfolded a few from the pile.

Kim was there to assist him.
The two had similar taste.
Both were divorced, with a child.
For Kim, there was no time to waste.

Jayson was very attentive.
Kim, happy he entered her life.
She met his daughter and he met Ben.
Kim hoped to become Jayson's wife.

But Jayson had other commitments.
His job interests always came first.
When he was transferred to L.A.,
by letter he told Kim the worst.

Very depressed by his kiss off,
Kim had thoughts of suicide.
But she also had Ben to think of.
He prevented her, before she tried.

In middle school, Ben failed his tests
and got in mischievous trouble.
When called to his Principal's office,
Kim burst her self-pity bubble.

"I have to climb out of my deep, dark abyss
and unplug my corked mindless fog."
Acknowledging that she needed some help,
Kim joined a small Synagogue.

At one of the congregant meetings,
Kim learned that without lots of money
she could live on a private kibbutz
in the holy Land of Milk and Honey.

Communal farm life intrigued Kim.
"A place Ben and I might discover
where we fit in the grand scheme of life,
with space for us both to recover."

Kim applied for their passports.
She studied all trip information.
She bought their El-Al airline tickets
and made their kibbutz reservation.

When he was told, Neil was incensed
in spite of his prior neglect.
"Too little, too late," was Kim's droll response.
His concern she chose to reject.

Neil was enraged and he slapped her.
He accused Kim of crossing his border,
then threatened to file a kidnapping charge.
Kim got a protective Court Order.

Neil was admonished, he had no claim
and at the Judge's behest,
Neil was required to pay back-support.
Noncompliance would mean his arrest.

As Kim and Ben packed their luggage,
her mom cried she'd miss them and grieve.
These words, meant as a guilt trip,
made Kim more determined to leave.

"Please visit," Kim called to her parents
as she boarded the flight, Israel bound.
And when the big jet safely landed,
Kim symbolically kissed the ground.

At the airport a pickup truck waited.
Off to the kibbutz it went.
"Richness for all in the Country,"
was this commune's ardent intent.

Kim and Ben got their assignments.
Kim's was to weed in the garden.
Ben was sent to the banana fields,
work to make his muscles harden.

Both of them learned to speak Hebrew.
This lifestyle filled them with glee.
Singing and dancing, and toiling the land
a stone's throw from the salty Dead Sea.

Approximately six months later,
Kim mailed her folks an invitation
to Ben's thirteenth birthday party
and his Bar Mitzvah celebration.

When Ben's big day had finally come
he stood healthy, triumphant, and tall
as he recited the Hebrew prayers
at the historical Western Wall.

Before they left, her mom and dad said
that they loved all of Kim's upbeat changes.
Once home, they swore, "We will visit again,"
in their infrequent phone call exchanges.

Of course, an obstacle always arose
whenever a trip was mentioned.
They made excuses, and so did Kim.
They all were well intentioned!

When Ben turned eighteen he was drafted
to serve with the Israeli troops.
With training and zeal he protected the Land
from invasion by unfriendly groups.

Kim sent her folks a photo of Ben
and the oversized Uzi he carried.
She also included one of herself
with the sexy Israeli she married.

GET MARRIED — BE JOYFUL

Tammy's folks were worrisome
with guilt-inducing fear
that they would not see Tammy wed.
This thought they could not bear.

"We want you to be happy,
to find true love and marry.
The burdens of our company
are ours and Jim's to carry."

Their shipping firm was fruitful.
The family was wealthy.
But there was sibling rivalry
that bordered on unhealthy.

Tammy's older brother Jim
worked in the firm since small,
expecting when he came of age
he would inherit all.

Tammy went to college,
but lacked skills for a career.
Marriage was expected,
but a spouse did not appear.

Her parents made an offer.
"Please, help out in the firm
until you find your calling.
Think of it as short term."

They each had their assignments.
Jim kept the ledger books.
Tammy wrote up orders
and watched out for the crooks.

Jim wasn't understanding.
He thought it was unfair.
*"I've worked hard to learn the trade.
Why should I have to share?"*

"We want you both to have success,"
their parents often said.
"To marry and have children,
not work here full of dread."

Their parents looked the other way
whenever they would fight.
*"If Tammy had a husband,
then things would be set right."*

So, brother-sister tension,
where push had turned to shove,
gave Tammy desperation
to go out and find love.

She met Bobby at a club.
He showed her sweet affection.
For Tammy, he was like a drug,
a smooth and rich confection.

Then, without forewarning,
Bobby disappeared.
Tammy called him with concern.
He told her what she feared.

He said that he was married
and had been, when they met.
"But I love you," he promised.
She told him not to fret.

She didn't tell him of her pain
nor did he see her cry.
She said that he could count on her.
When he did, she would comply.

Throughout his many conquests,
for Bobby she was there
ignoring his thickheaded words
she didn't want to hear.

The years flew by so quickly.
The days were all the same.
Tammy stuck in her folks' firm
with marriage still her aim.

Then one day Tammy's life changed
by an out-of-control truck
that sped along the highway.
Her parents' car was struck.

Her brother Jim was driving.
Her family was killed.
Tammy now was owner of
their shipping firm, as willed.

Bobby now saw reason
to divorce his wife.
Tammy said, "Good riddance!"
and sliced him from her life.

She took a cruise, where she met Tom
who helped her grieving mend.
Unlike Bobby, Tom became
her partner and best friend.

Deep in commerce, Tom exported
heavy pipes of lead.
Tammy's shipping firm shipped pipes!
Soon after they were wed.

They had a son and named him Jim.
Her folks would have been thrilled
to see their dream for Tammy
so joyously fulfilled.

REFLECTION — AFFECTION

She was a pricey showgirl,
a high-kicking, dancing Rockette.
She knew all the moves to entice men,
but totally lacked etiquette.

Gary was born out of wedlock.
Her career went on hold, for his sake.
When asked who his dad was, she told him,
"He was my best, one-night stand, mistake."

She'd take Gary with her to the theater
and point to their mirror-reflection.
"There you are, Gary, clutching my arm.
That's a show of our love and affection."

She taught Gary to be conniving
and told him how he must react.
"Never show your disappointment.
When sad, do a credible act."

So, Gary became a trained actor.
Due to his mother's great need,
Gary was sent to performing arts schools.
"My gift, so that you will succeed."

She often would show him old pictures
of herself, when in her prime,
with emphasis on all she gave up.
For that, he owed her, big time!

Because of his good looks and talent
Gary was given a part
in TV, movies, and Theater.
For an actor, this was a great start.

From Broadway out to Hollywood,
with no time to digress,
Gary, only seventeen,
fell for a hot actress.

He wanted love, she gave him sex.
Most times, her squeals were pretended.
When Gary's mom caught wind of the two,
their romantic fling swiftly ended.

The next epic film Gary starred in,
he knocked up a young beauty queen.
His mother paid for her abortion.
The girl was not even sixteen.

His mother banked most of his earnings.
The large amount, she would grandstand.
Until Gary was twenty-one plus,
he was forced to obey her command.

"If you do everything that I say
exactly as you are told,
you will have not only glory
but a big, heavy pot filled with gold."

So, Gary learned to define glory
as the love that his mother held back.
He thought when he had the money
then nothing out there would he lack.

Yet even when Gary reached every goal
and followed her rules to the letter,
regardless of how full his pot of gold was,
his mom told him he could do better.

On his twenty-first birthday, Gary knew
he was burnt out from being onstage.
*"I'd rather be behind the scenes
without a high-pressure gauge."*

He shared these feelings with his mom
and told her what he planned.
"I will be a casting agent.
Still showbiz, but not as grand."

"This business role lacks grandeur,"
his mom sulked in despair.
"Your name won't make the headlines
as a run-of-the-mill millionaire."

But she went with him to restaurants
where the rich were known to eat
and applauded when he bought a ranch,
two cars, and a penthouse suite.

Then, one day on his way to work,
he got caught in a torrential rain.
Not carrying his tote umbrella,
Gary jumped on the Express A Train.

When he reached his destination
a spitfire passed by his eye.
He stopped her from leaving the station
until there was blue in the sky.

Marlyrose was Hispanic,
exotic, quick-witted, and tough.
She'd been in the States just over a year
and finding employment was rough.

She said she grew up in poverty,
the eldest child of eight.
"My mother died when I was fourteen.
My dad drank, and drunk, came home late."

"When back in Guatemala,
I was a cook, nanny, and servant.
My boss, a highly paid diplomat,
recognized I was more than observant."

"He paid my way to the U.S.A.
for me to study a trade.
I am enrolled in business school
to no longer be somebody's maid."

So when Marlyrose met Gary
she recognized he was her chance
to broaden and raise her horizons
and also to have some romance.

Attracted to her deep copper skin,
Gary was purely elated
to find a woman who lifted him up.
With her, he did not feel deflated.

She laughed when he made silly jokes
and helped him gain more confidence.
After a few weeks of dating,
Marlyrose moved into his residence.

Marlyrose proved she could be
a solid and steady right-hand
by helping Gary with his constant work
and meeting its rigid demand.

Both reaped rewards from this union.
It was healthy and naturally seized.
Until Gary's mom claimed her usual stance,
"Gary, I am so displeased!"

She feared the truth. That Marlyrose
was not just a fast-passing whim.
In keeping with her *"rights as a mom,"*
she used guilt to manipulate him.

"I'll make sure that she is deported
unless you swear to stay apart."
This time, Gary stood up strongly
and candidly spoke from his heart.

He told his mother, "Stop your games.
They prove that you are nuts."
Then Gary married Marlyrose
to show that he had guts.

Five great years together,
Marlyrose craved a baby.
Gary feared his life would change.
In response he promised, "Maybe."

Though both made a sincere attempt,
Gary was relieved
that time flew by and Marlyrose
still had not conceived.

They went to see a doctor
who said their chance was none.
"The only way you'll have a child
is by adopting one."

They signed up with an agency,
and then dismissed the thought.
*"Adoption takes so many years,
our chance, likely, is naught."*

Their lives continued as they were.
Hard work followed by play.
Until they got a phone call
on that fateful warm spring day.

Their lawyer at the agency
had come upon a case
where a teenager gave up her son.
The baby was mixed race.

Baby Marco came that week.
They both were unprepared.
Marlyrose was overawed
and Gary clearly scared.

His attitude caused conflict.
Gary was depressed.
"This whole thing happened
much too fast," Marlyrose confessed.

Gary wanted pampering
that Marco now was getting.
While Marlyrose was mothering,
Gary stood by fretting.

Or he spent the weekdays
in their New York penthouse suite,
while Marlyrose and Marco stayed
in their ranch house retreat.

On weekends, when he visited,
his mother came along.
She'd coo to grandson Marco
then tell Gary what was wrong.

"Marlyrose is classless.
She wed you for your wealth.
Now that she has a child to raise,
forget about your health!"

When Gary didn't fight his mom
and stand up for his wife
the ultimatum came his way.
"Get HER out of your life!"

Alas, the "HER" was Marlyrose.
She filed for divorce.
Gary's mother had won the war.
There was no good recourse.

The ranch house went to Marlyrose
as part of her alimony.
Gary was princely with child support
and even bought Marco a pony.

With Marlyrose and Marco gone,
Gary's mother was thrilled.
She had her son to put on display,
and Gary's need was fulfilled.

Together they'd go to the theater.
She'd point to their mirror-reflection.
"There you are, Gary, clutching my arm.
That's a show of our love and affection."

BASEBALL WITH MY SON

Roger and Cheryl met in school,
a small college in the Midwest.
Cheryl grew up in that quaint rural town
but Roger was far from his nest.

Roger was a native New Yorker.
Yankee Stadium was near his home.
As a kid he'd go to the games with his dad.
In his mind, he would go there and roam.

His dad was a traveling salesman.
None of his time could be spared.
Only when Roger would talk about sports
did his dad demonstrate that he cared.

Roger's mom was a housewife.
As such, she was fully compliant.
With Roger, however, she towed the line
and taught him to be self-reliant.

She made sure Roger excelled in school
so that when his dad was around
he would have knowledge about many things.
But baseball was their common ground.

Roger, a scribbler by instinct
loved to critique every game.
He'd jot down his choices to share with his dad,
but their picks were never the same.

"Why don't you write a book," his dad said,
dismissive and somewhat demeaning.
Roger decided that one day he would
show his dad the strength of his leaning.

That's why Roger went to this school.
It taught analytical skills.
Roger's goal now was to write about sports
in a way that would pay all his bills.

Cheryl aspired to marry a man
with talent and lots of ambition.
Roger fulfilled her requirements well,
except when it came to tradition.

Willing to bring Cheryl along,
that is if she wanted to go,
Roger set ground rules before she said, "Yes."
To commitment, Roger said, "No."

Cheryl loved Roger, so she acquiesced.
"I really have nothing to lose.
I've always wanted to live in New York.
On marriage, I'll change Roger's views!"

So they came East, and Roger was hired
as a sportswriter, as planned.
Cheryl found work in an office.
For a while, she made no demand.

Her goal was to have a husband,
and a child to wheel in a carriage.
But Roger was not in a hurry
for Cheryl to hook him in marriage.

Five years passed, still no commitment.
Sick of his self-centered need
Cheryl threatened to walk out the door.
That's when Roger agreed.

No other woman he'd met filled his void.
Only Cheryl had answered his call.
They wed in the courthouse during lunch break,
and that night, on TV, watched baseball.

To offset the years Cheryl waited,
in nine months, she gave birth to their son.
While Roger spent more time at his job,
she had their household to run.

Roger, who'd been so creative
now handed most writing work down.
As his staff grew, Roger traveled around
to the sporting events out of town.

Cheryl made sure to remind him
that he'd taken a page from his dad.
Whenever their son sought attention,
Roger spoke of the latest sports fad.

Disheartened by Roger's behavior,
Cheryl became more commanding.
Then, without warning, Roger's dad died.
For Roger, the world was disbanding.

Facing the truth, Roger saw how his worth
was measured by what he could prove.
This reckoning gave him the impetus
to finally break from his groove.

He quit his job shortly thereafter.
Then with his son and his wife
Roger returned to the small college town
to restructure their new way of life.

As a family now going forward,
Cheryl was pleased with the past.
Now she urged Roger to write his memoir,
"Baseball with My Son ... at Last."

SILVER SPOON

Todd grew up in Hollywood.
Born with a silver spoon,
his parents bought him everything.
Their limit was the moon.

His mother was an actress
in the glamour girl tradition.
His father was a self-important,
L.A. cosmetician.

They were divorced when Todd was two.
Custody was shared.
His mom spent her time making films.
His dad's concern, impaired.

Todd's childhood was rowdy
without much supervision.
Most of his education
came from watching television.

His friends were sons and daughters
of famous movie stars.
With them he tossed around a ball,
went surfing, and raced cars.

Like many of his cohorts
whose homelife wasn't strong,
Todd followed all trends, briefly.
He stayed with nothing long.

Todd rarely got direction.
His parents didn't care.
They gave him everything in vogue.
They said, "We did our share."

What Todd had really wanted
were their kisses and warm hugs.
But they were not forthcoming.
Todd replaced their love with drugs.

A joint of marijuana
at first got him quite high.
But soon that wasn't adequate.
He needed more to fly.

He found his mom's prescriptions
and started popping pills.
Uppers, downers, he used all,
then got some more refills.

Any drug that filled his void
Todd was keen to try.
He soon abused all opiates,
the best money could buy.

DENA STEWART

The headline in the tabloids read,
"Todd Tried to Reach the Moon."
Found on his lifeless body
was his *silver* cocaine *spoon*.

GIRLHOOD FRIENDS

They grew up in the 60s
when students made much noise.
But rather than political,
their focus was on boys.

When demonstrations were the norm
and life was one big riot,
they were more concerned with clothes
and every new fad diet.

The four best friends did nothing
without checking with each other.
They were so inseparable
they could have had one mother.

They all went on to college.
Their goal was good careers.
They tested murky waters
as they overcame their fears.

They traveled and they dated,
and swore they'd let no man
get in the way of friendship.
The first to go was Fran.

Fran met Gerald at a dance.
They married right away.
Her first born came within nine months.
Fran had no time to play.

Ivy was the next to leave
to another state.
There, at grad school she met Kent.
"Our love will not abate!"

Dee and Jody stayed behind.
Then Jody made her move.
She said she needed distance
until she found her groove.

Jody's groove was Edgar,
quite rich and erudite.
When introduced, he scoffed at Dee.
Dee split rather than fight.

Ivy visited Dee once,
but Ivy acted strange.
She and Kent were just divorced
and Ivy dreaded change.

Dee heard from Fran shortly before
Dee and Lou were married.
"Sorry I'll miss your wedding,
but I'm pregnant and too harried."

The years flew by. Dee's life was full.
She thought about old friends.
She missed what she remembered
of those trusting dividends.

One day, by sheer coincidence,
Dee saw Jody's old neighbor
who said she'd heard from Jody's mom.
"Jody was in labor."

"She's expecting her first child.
For her age, that is late.
But she and Edgar have the means.
They own a large estate."

Dee then saw Ivy's sister.
"Ivy earned her Ph.D.
She's remarried to a realtor
with a law degree."

"Fran raised two sons, both doctors,"
according to Fran's dad,
who Dee bumped into on the street.
Dee told him she was glad.

"So all my friends found glory,"
was what Dee had surmised.
This caused Dee to look inward.
"Have I compromised?"

"My resume's erratic.
I left that old rat race
to become a writer.
A whim I still embrace."

"And Lou's an edgy artist.
As such, we aren't wealthy.
But we're rich in inspiration
and the food we eat is healthy."

"We chose not to have children,
so had time to follow trends.
I'm satisfied with what I have!"
Dee emailed her three friends.

She sent them invitations
to a restaurant they all knew.
To share some poignant memories,
have snacks, and down a brew.

Fran was the first one to arrive,
Ivy and Jody followed.
Before they spoke, they ordered drinks,
all took a gulp and swallowed.

There was an awkward silence
as they checked each other out.
They all began to speak at once,
then stopped rather than shout.

Dee hoped they'd let their guard down,
and relive their once close past.
Tell stories of the fun they had,
see why it didn't last.

Well, Ivy bragged about her gains
and Jody condescended.
Fran showed pictures of her kids.
Abruptly, their lunch ended.

As they hugged they all agreed
to meet again, real soon.
But it appeared that each of them
danced to a different tune.

Years ago when they split up,
each blamed it on the men.
But this reunion proved the point,
"You can't go home again!"

ODE TO A GRECIAN SUNBURN

Ellen was exhausted.
As a lawyer she worked hard.
Her boyfriend cheated then skipped town.
Her feelings were still scarred.

When Kate, a prosecutor,
said, "Let's go on vacation,"
Ellen was delighted.
She agreed, no trepidation.

Ellen knew with time away
she'd find her inner peace.
"What finer place to sort things out
than on the coast of Greece?"

Four days before they were to leave
Kate was assigned a case.
Not wanting to thwart Ellen's plans,
Kate's friend Meg took her place.

Ellen met Meg just once before.
Their interests, far apart.
They agreed to share a room,
dodge unease from the start.

The first day worked out pretty well,
but nighttime caused great tension.
Meg brought back a stranger,
with zero prior mention.

So Ellen moved from their hotel
to a cottage near the beach.
Wary of being alone, at first,
she liked having no one in reach.

As Ellen basked in the burning sun
and leafed through Vogue magazine,
she noticed the most magnificent male
compared to all others she'd seen.

He was a sculptured Grecian God,
blue eyes and thick blonde hair.
And when he flexed his biceps
Ellen could not help but stare.

She didn't make it obvious,
but when she caught his eye
he waved to her, flashed a grin,
and then meandered by.

John was from San Diego,
the star of a theater troupe.
This was his last day in Mykonos
before meeting up with his group.

John asked Ellen to join him
in a lengthy leisurely walk.
They strode the tree-lined pathways
for deep psychological talk.

He brought out Ellen's wild side.
Her dream was to be much looser.
His was to be a screenwriter
or theatrical Broadway producer.

They ate and drank, they danced and sang.
They basked in the rapture they felt.
Back in Ellen's ethereal suite
their bodies, so hot, seemed to melt.

Engulfed in sweaty ardor
as both of them reached a new height,
they held each other tightly
the remainder of that starry night.

Their parting wasn't tearful,
they both had gotten pleasure.
For Ellen, a perfect romance
and a memory to treasure.

When Ellen returned to New York
and resumed the rigors of life,
she met and fell in love with Steve.
One year later, she became his wife.

Steve was an FBI man.
Together they were "Law & Order."
Yet, in between long hours and work
they had a beautiful daughter.

She quickly grew, and off she went
to a college considered the best.
Ellen and Steve were now all alone
in their cluttered, dull, empty nest.

They talked about retiring,
then bickered about money.
What once made Ellen laugh out loud
she no longer found to be funny.

Their sex life turned to boredom,
divorce crossed Ellen's mind.
But Steve was understanding
and never left her behind.

In his attempt to make her smile
and surprise her on her birthday,
Steve bought two rare tickets
for a hit show playing Broadway.

Leafing through her program,
right there on the front page
were the names of all the folks
who brought this play to stage.

The director, and the lighting crew,
of course, the acting cast.
The producer with his picture
had his credits listed last.

Ellen felt her heart race
remembering their passion.
He was in the audience
in current theater fashion.

She spotted him; he now was old,
his blonde hair, silver gray.
When John turned his head around,
Ellen did not look away.

Their eyes connected briefly.
She sensed his recognition.
But, before they locked their gaze
John shifted his position.

His glance brought back sensations
of sexual desire.
Her mind now filled with fantasy,
her body was afire.

Throughout the long performance
she daydreamed about Greece.
By the time it ended,
Ellen had found calming peace.

When Steve asked if she liked the show,
she answered, "It was grand."
And as they left the theater
Ellen squeezed her husband's hand.

THE LITTLE WOOD FLUTE

Otto was born in Germany
in nineteen thirty-nine,
and raised in a pastoral village
very close to the Rhine.

Eva and Klaus, Otto's parents,
owned a small music shoppe.
When the Nazis came into power
their finances took a big drop.

Eva and Klaus were determined
to take an affirmative stand.
They did what they could, and with others
resisted Hitler's command.

They secretly helped many people
escape from brutal S.S. troops.
They opened up their cramped basement
to hide several victimized groups.

When Gestapo forces searched houses,
their underground place was discovered.
Eva and Klaus were taken away.
Their bodies were never recovered.

The boys who Otto escaped with
subsisted on berries and fruit.
At night, when despair overcame them,
Otto played his little wood flute.

His papa had carved the instrument.
For Otto, the sounds gave him hope.
Music eased his crippling fear
enabling him, somehow, to cope.

When the war was finally over
Otto wandered onto a farm
owned by an elderly widow.
She promised to keep him from harm.

Greta warmed Otto and fed him.
She nurtured his musical bent.
He was given a good education
at the prep school, to which he was sent.

Later on, he went to college.
He earned credits in music and art.
Otto was trained to be skillful.
Academically, Otto was smart.

Soon after his graduation,
Greta died in her sleep.
For the first time since the war ended,
Otto was able to weep.

Too many memories tugged at his heart,
so Otto decided to leave.
He sold Greta's house and farmland
and left Deutschland on New Year's Eve.

He arrived in New York with a big metal trunk
containing his books and one suit.
He wore a sports shirt and wrinkle free slacks,
in his pocket, his little wood flute.

From a print ad, he found an apartment
and settled in quickly enough.
Though he had all the credentials,
finding a job was more tough.

So rather than seeking employment,
with his money he rented a store
and turned it into a music shoppe,
the kind he had known once before.

He stocked it with musical instruments
and sheet music from foreign lands,
as well as American Blues and Jazz,
and records by popular bands.

Most of his time he spent working.
Loneliness, Otto ignored.
When he was sad, he played his wood flute.
Otto claimed he never was bored.

One day a young woman entered his shoppe.
She appeared to be Otto's age.
With long blond hair, pink cheeks, blue eyes —
a face that belonged on the stage.

She skimmed through the racks and selected
an album of German folk songs.
She said, "They remind me of those whom I lost.
My way to keep memories strong."

Otto was instantly smitten,
and Lena was willing to talk.
Soon the time came to lock up his store.
Otto did, and they went for a walk.

They headed to a famous Brauhaus
in Yorkville, known as Germantown.
There they sipped Lager with bratwursts,
which Lena and Otto wolfed down.

At first they just spoke of the present.
Then Lena told Otto her tale
of sorrow, fear, and great tragic loss,
and all that she did to prevail.

"My family hid in a basement.
They were found and taken away.
As a girl of just ten my life was spared
but I had a big price to pay."

"Because I was pretty to look at,
they pressured me to entertain
the commanding Nazi officials.
I sang songs about spirit and gain."

"After the war, now teen-age,
I was found by a distant relation.
She made sure I had shelter and food
and was given a good education."

"When I was older and out on my own,
I was hired to work for an airline.
The passengers lifted my spirits
when I went on a mood-swing decline."

Wanting to know more, Otto asked,
"Is New York your base when not flying?"
"It is," Lena said. "But the pain of my youth
gives me nightmares that wake me up crying."

Otto took Lena home late that night,
aware now how empty he'd been.
Always the proper gentleman,
he was glad she invited him in.

Her two-room apartment was tasteful.
Serious art, nothing cute.
Otto's eyes popped when he noticed her desk,
and on it a little wood flute.

Lena told Otto the flute was a gift
from a man who had carved just one more.
"His son had the other, but he likely died.
This all happened during the war."

Astounded and dazed by her statement,
Otto stood still as a rock.
Unable to move or utter a sound,
so solid was his state of shock.

Lena stared at him with wonder.
She had no idea what was wrong.
Guessing it had to do with the flute,
she started to play a folk song.

The tune, Otto knew from his childhood
and hearing it made his tears flow.
He took out his flute from his pocket.
Without words, he let Lena know.

He was the son of that musical man,
the one who had helped save her life.
Though she kept her job with the airline
Lena became Otto's wife.

Now when their past is remembered
they talk of their commingled roots
and their serendipitous meeting.
Together, they play their wood flutes.

NO CLUE!

David's parents owned a Deli
where local groups would meet.
The varied menu offered food
that everyone could eat.

They worked seven days a week
while standing on their feet.
At home his dad was grouchy
so David would retreat.

His dad railed at him to read
and be well-educated.
But David had dyslexia
which made this complicated.

This handicap caused David's dad
to call him dense and lazy.
As an adolescent,
his dad would yell, "You're crazy!"

David really was quite smart.
He had a funny style.
He covered up his anguish
with his contagious smile.

His last year in middle school,
David acted out.
He became a tough boy
instead of a Boy Scout.

In the Bronx, where they lived,
the street gangs had long reach.
That's when David's family
uprooted to Long Beach.

David entered high school,
more competitive than most.
His dad opened a restaurant.
His mother served as host.

Every day after school
David helped his folks.
In school he was the punchline
of all his classmates' jokes.

During breaks, the guys he knew,
all had exotic plans,
while David's dad had David
in the kitchen scraping pans.

"This business will be yours," he said,
each time David complained.
But David had his own plans,
not this restaurant, as ordained.

The summer of his senior year,
David was defiant.
He quit his family's business
to be more self-reliant.

He got a job at a hotel
that served the upper-class.
He emulated what he saw.
No longer was he crass.

His dad oozed with resentment.
He cursed the rich hotel
for influencing David
into thinking he'd excel.

"You're a loser," his dad snarled,
like talking to a rival,
ignoring David's growing need
for space and self-survival.

When David tried to help him out,
his dad replied with wrath,
"How dare you think you're better
than me, or my chosen path."

When David grumbled to his mom,
she took his father's side.
"Your dad told me he's proud of you."
His meanness, she denied.

When David finished high school
he refused to be held down.
He used his own saved money
for college out of town.

He joined a large fraternity
and made some good new friends.
His major was in business
and how to market trends.

While there, he met Christina.
She had issues with her mother.
"Chris" and David married,
giving balance to each other.

Returning to Manhattan
after graduation,
David launched a PR firm
seeking accreditation.

Anticipating criticism,
David was amazed
that his clients were content
and his hard work was praised.

Chris was in Advertising.
She was a copywriter.
Together, Chris and David
often pulled an overnighter.

When in his middle thirties,
David yearned to be on stage.
"To be a different person,
let loose, forget his age."

Chris said, "Go Audition,
tryout and take a chance."
He was cast to play the lead
in a thriller romance.

His role required shouting.
His image was his dad.
David recalled all the ways
his dad made him feel bad.

The audience believed him.
Critics showed admiration.
His father scoffed at his reviews
with hurtful deprecation.

Invited to the celebration
for this small hit show,
David wished his castmates fun,
but he refused to go.

Chris astutely pointed out
that every time he'd win,
he'd minimize his efforts
as if triumph was a sin.

David knew why victory
made him feel afraid.
Each time he gained, his father lost.
Guilt was the price he paid.

Chris urged him to face his dad,
"Be honest, that's the cure."
But when dad saw blame coming,
he stormed right out the door.

Time went by without amends.
His dad got sick and died.
With very mixed emotions,
in private David cried.

When his grief subsided,
with no cause to refrain,
he visited his mother
to share with her his pain.

He thought that with his dad gone,
she'd want to reconnect.
He craved her validation
and hoped for her respect.

He quoted his dad's hurtful words.
His mom said, "That's a lie!
You created discord
when you would not comply."

She maintained what she believed,
his dad's point of view.
David calmly stated,
"You're one mother with no clue!"

Now David's firm is thriving.
He, sometimes, is an actor.
He's learned to like his victories.
"Be gone, ego detractor!"

MONEY, MISERY, MIRACLE

Carly was born into money.
Her father invested in land.
Fetching and smooth, all the women he wooed,
jumped at his every demand.

When Carly was young, her parents divorced.
Mom caught dad in bed with her friend.
With cringe-worthy mean retribution,
their marriage then came to an end.

Dad paid Carly's mom alimony,
a court-ordered unfair amount.
As per their written agreement
Carly had her own bank account.

Her dad was her Superhero.
She viewed him with childlike awe.
But as she grew older he came around less.
Carly thought that was due to her flaw.

She masked her hurt with dark humor,
being glib, sarcastic, and funny.
Often jesting that she would trade love
for all of her father's guilt-money.

As a teenager, Carly was curvy.
"You look like a tramp," her mom yelled.
So Carly flaunted her assets.
She ignored her mom's gibes, and rebelled.

She went to an Ivy League college
to learn the best ways to compete.
But Carly preferred unkempt hippies
to the snobbery of the elite.

With free love the trend, she got pregnant.
Her dad said that she was disgusting.
As punishment he cut her credit.
Desperation now sprung from her lusting.

Her mother showed her no comfort.
Abortion was Carly's best option.
Instead, she gave birth to a sweet baby girl.
The child was put up for adoption.

"One day, I'll be somebody's mother,"
was a thought that brought Carly enjoyment.
Her next step was to win back her dad's goodwill.
For that, she needed employment.

She knew most of her Dad's connections
and politely asked him to arrange
an interview with Jack, his broker,
down at the New York Stock Exchange.

Jack managed a sizable hedge fund.
In his field he was greatly admired
for his depth of resourceful shrewdness.
Instantly, Carly was hired.

She had a crush on fast talking Jack.
Jack saw he could toy with her heart.
"Her daddy's wealth one day will be hers,
and mine, if I play this game smart."

So Jack proposed and they married.
Their union delighted her dad,
"I really hope she'll be happy."
He was unaware Jack was a cad.

As a couple, the two ran all over town.
On Jack, Carly would dote.
With funds her dad had invested,
Jack gave Carly gems and a mink coat.

Then, she told Jack it was time to have kids.
Jack said, "No! I want to travel."
He blamed all their woes on her nagging.
Jack's pretense began to unravel.

Jack's scorn for Carly grew hurtful.
It fueled her sense of degradation.
Her only ask was to have a child,
which failed Jack's consideration.

Carly suggested they separate,
but to her horrific dismay,
Jack said, "No one could love you like I do!
So, NO! I demand that you stay."

Mentally whipped, she had no place to go
and maintain her slick lavish style.
For twenty years she lived with Jack,
fully aware he was vile.

Then one day, she got the call.
Her father, quite old now, had died.
To Carly, he willed his entire estate,
leaving her amply supplied.

But this vast wealth pained Carly more
when she overheard her husband scheming
to cause her death in an accident
where no one would hear her loud screaming.

In fear for her life, Carly sensibly hired
an attorney and a detective.
"Find dirt on Jack to get my divorce!"
was Carly's frantic directive.

Jack had bamboozled his clients.
He was tried, and sent off to jail.
Carly was now a free woman
with resources, and an itch to prevail.

She used her upscale education
to invest her wealth in some land.
On it she built a brick safehouse
with plans to quickly expand.

As captain of her own vast empire,
Carly needed an assistant.
A person with good managerial skills,
trustworthy and very consistent.

Carly read applications.
Most had a long cover letter.
Only one stood out from the rest.
Four words, "May we get together?"

Her name was Beth, age twenty-one.
Carly had a positive hunch.
She called the phone number on the note
and asked Beth to meet her for lunch.

Carly was slightly late to arrive.
Beth was about to be seated.
Her tent dress embellished a pregnancy bump.
For a moment, Carly's mind retreated.

As she took her place at the table,
Carly thought of what she had lost
when she gave up her child for adoption.
Regret was her high-interest cost.

Which led Carly to instantly ask,
"Do you need work and hope to be hired?"
Beth shook her head and slowly explained
what it was that she truly desired.

"My husband is very supportive
and my parents are better than great.
With the baby due in less than two months,
they urged me to set up this date."

"I've known all along I'm adopted,
but my birth records had been a mystery.
With DNA tracing I've finally learned
of my, once sealed, genetic history."

Years before, Carly had supplied
saliva for her DNA test.
"If ever, by chance, I am searched for …,"
was her fantasy thought, made in jest.

Back to what Beth had been saying
without any equivocation,
"It appears that you're my birth mother."
Carly responded with pure exultation.

"You are my beautiful daughter!
I've dreamed of this day, every day.
I'm jubilant that you have found me.
If you'll let me, my wish is to stay."

Six weeks later, Beth had her baby.
Carly's devotion was instant.
She blissfully babysits for her grandchild,
and Beth is her loyal assistant.

THE TOWER

His dad collected garbage
for city sanitation.
For Fred, he wanted the reverse —
clean clothes and admiration.

He worked for his son's future
and believed Fred would comply
to having higher goals than his.
"Build towers towards the sky."

Engrained in Fred were his dad's words,
"Do not become a centrist.
Never settle for middling.
Be a doctor or a dentist."

So Fred became a dentist,
but felt his obligation
was in military service.
Payback for education.

Infuriated was his dad
that Fred would choose that path.
"You'll end up dead or ostracized,"
he yelled at Fred, with wrath.

As part of a M.A.S.H. unit
to use his dental skill,
Fred was sent to Kabul.
There he saw soldiers kill.

Deep inside a combat zone,
firsthand Fred witnessed war.
Men he knew and treated, died
before they could withdraw.

After his rough tour ended,
when newly back in town,
Fred's father started goading him,
"It's time you settle down."

Fred's folks did not commend him
for his wartime sacrifice.
When Fred revealed the horrors,
they begged, "Don't be so precise."

So Fred rented an office
and denied his pent-up sorrow.
His dad was buoyant, Fred was safe.
"This way you'll see tomorrow!"

A toothache forced Liz to call Fred.
It needed to be treated.
The root canal procedure took
six weeks until completed.

Accompanied by laughing gas
and Novocain injection,
Liz and Fred connected
with a chemical affection.

Liz was a social climber.
Fred's dad was very proud
when Fred and Liz were married
and Fred joined her monied crowd.

Her dad, a wealthy landlord,
leased a large array
of city suites and country homes
for his rich friends to stay.

He let Fred use an office
with an Avenue address.
Cosmetic dentistry fit in
with Fred's goal, to impress.

Fred tasted all the perks of wealth,
but had no time for fun.
And matters only worsened
when Liz had their baby son.

Liz had a Nanny watch him
while she idly lunched with friends.
She shopped and went to health spas,
buying into all new trends.

Dentistry, precise and dull
gave Fred no motivation.
He dwelled on wartime combat
when loud blasts were stimulation.

Fred's city practice fell apart.
He chose to live upstate.
An obsession for equipment
began to elevate.

Fred bought large machines and trucks,
and heavy tools with power.
On their rural property,
Fred built himself a tower.

From there, he shouted orders.
They mostly were ignored,
diminishing Fred's value.
"Please help me," Fred implored.

Liz aimed to be supportive,
but Fred's fury turned demeaning.
Her solace could not calm him
as he'd twist its offered meaning.

Expanding his collection,
Fred bought an army tank
and dressed up in his uniform
when Captain was his rank.

Fearing what Fred might do next
Liz cautiously did tread.
But P.T.S.D. had kicked in.
Fred slid back, not ahead.

He now relied on alcohol
to numb his desperation.
"Please see a doctor," Liz cajoled.
"You need strong medication."

"You'll lose your worth if muddied.
Think bold or end up hurt,"
were words that swirled around Fred's mind
as he dug mounds of dirt.

Then Fred climbed his high tower
and used his machine gun
to finalize his battle.
Fred killed his wife and son.

Enmeshed in scathing anguish,
caught up in sheer disgrace
Fred ended his own torment
with a bullet to his face.

"I'm sorry, Dad, I let you down
and plunged into depression.
I tried my best to reach the sky,"
read Fred's written confession.

A BIG BUST

He'd been a high-priced lawyer,
his clients, mostly ratified.
John retired from his Firm
when no longer gratified.

He had this midlife crisis
when barely forty-five.
Working in an office
decreased John's will to strive.

He yearned for an adventure:
"To leave his comfort zone.
To try things that were dangerous.
To shake up his drab tone."

So John became a city cop
assigned to several stations.
His job was to protect and serve,
and write up violations.

Older than most rookies
when he joined the Force,
John recognized the swindlers,
and the rules he could enforce.

His wife of ten years left him.
She loathed his new profession.
To her, his lower paycheck
was a social transgression.

This day began quite normally.
John did his six-mile run.
He shaved, then donned his uniform
and loaded his big gun.

He went to morning roll call
and received his daily beat —
the Westside subway station
and its surrounding street.

John walked along the platform.
He checked the subway riders.
He collared a pickpocket
and smiled at rule abiders.

He had a nose for trouble.
She was pretty but looked tough,
the type to undermine the law
then say, "The cop got rough."

She carried a small suitcase
for maybe a short trip,
as well as a large handbag
that she balanced on her hip.

John watched her scan the crowd size
before squeezing through the gate
without a transit pass or card.
John had no time to wait.

He walked up and confronted her.
She sneered and moved away.
John commanded that she stay,
but she would not obey.

John put her wrists in handcuffs.
He asked for information.
She refused to answer, so —
down to the police station.

There, John learned Dale was a narc
about to make a bust.
By not blowing her cover,
her street creds stayed robust.

She'd been after a dealer
who was heading towards the train
when John was making his arrest
and forced her to refrain.

At thirty-eight, Dale looked young.
John had been deceived.
But doing his job by the book
Dale's act had been believed.

Dale was a seasoned officer,
who found danger conducive.
But as a woman in this field
upgrades were still elusive.

So John was brought into the case.
The next day, Dale was back.
They nabbed the dealer jointly
with two, five-pound bags of crack.

For aiding Dale in this arrest,
John earned a new position
as a plainclothes detective.
Great for his disposition!

Dale thought John "intriguing"
for following his passion.
*"Dressing up in Navy Blue
instead of high-end fashion."*

Due to his legal background,
John quickly moved ahead.
He outranks Dale, but when at home,
he's handcuffed to their bed!

SALVATION

As Simon's health was failing
Jay began to wonder,
*"Where do souls of the righteous go
when the body is six feet under?"*

Jay was Simon's grandson.
Simon, a scholar and sage,
gave Jay noble wisdom
at a youthful, trusting age.

When Jay turned thirteen, Simon said,
"Do gracious deeds, and serve.
To be let into heaven
you must strictly observe."

Jay's mom, Simon's daughter,
respected his position.
But she raised Jay Agnostic,
with no shred of contrition.

Jay lived in Manhattan,
with friends from many lands.
He saw varied traditions
but followed no demands.

Simon was from Poland.
His folks were persecuted.
Their dignity was stripped away,
their properties were looted.

Simon fled to America
where riches were achieved.
A place to join the melting pot
and pray as one believed.

Simon was most self-assured
with those who shared his views.
He joined a place of worship
with ultra-Orthodox Jews.

He practiced all the written laws.
The Bible, he debated.
With other scholars he discussed
how mankind was created.

He was ordained a Rabbi,
then proclaimed as a scribe.
By hand, he penned a Torah
and wrote books about each tribe.

When Simon thought to marry,
a broker chose his match.
Known as a man of wisdom
made Simon a good catch.

His wife was quite devoted.
They had daughters and sons.
The girls were barred from having dolls,
the boys could have no guns.

"Toys distract from learning.
Ignorance is a flaw.
And dolls are little idols,
forbidden in Orthodox law."

These were among the reasons
Jay's mom spurned these positions.
Simon wouldn't praise her
unless she met his conditions.

Simon had a way with words,
such as, "The gain of sacrifice —
It helps accept cruel tragedies
when common sense would not suffice."

"Religion teaches tolerance
and basic understanding
of what it means to pray to God
when life seems too demanding."

When Simon's wife, Jay's grandma, died,
he said, "It was God's right.
God makes a life, God takes a life.
God's powers are all might."

The years went by. His offspring grew.
Most maintained honest living.
Simon now spent all his time
praying and thanks giving.

Jay, a tax accountant,
observed no Jewish ritual.
He overcame his hurdles
without making prayers habitual.

Until that night, he had four beers,
then rammed a car's behind.
Jay walked away with a cracked rib,
bringing God to mind.

"Be grateful that you are alive
and didn't have to bleed
to know that you were lucky.
Rejoice! Don't drink or speed."

Euphoria for Jay soon ebbed,
his piety put aside.
While driving drunk he swiped a dog.
Jay thought, for sure, it died.

It wasn't God he saw this time.
Jay had a new concern.
"What if my grandfather was right?
Am I doomed to Hell to burn?"

"If the only ones in heaven
are those faithful to observe,
is there hope for folks like me?
Can I unbend my curve?"

Jay wanted reassurance that
his fate could be reversed.
"If I repent, can I erase
forever being cursed?"

But on his deathbed, Simon wailed,
scared of his own damnation!
Leaving Jay to question,
"Who decrees recrimination?"

A MATTER OF CHOICE

Jane lived in New York City,
but her relatives were reclusive.
Jane's dream was to be unrestricted,
independent and exclusive.

Jane's parents had some education.
Her mother was set in her ways.
Her father, a self-righteous zealot,
preached Bible verse to all the strays.

He stayed far from family matters.
In his spare time he slept or he prayed.
He never had time to play with his kids,
yet, his orders, his children obeyed.

So growing up was problematic.
Jane didn't excel when in school.
And her folks used rigid moral constraints
to force her to follow each rule.

But godliness wasn't Jane's calling.
She wanted more options to choose,
which, of course, her folks wouldn't hear of.
What Jane wanted, she had to lose.

Disgruntled with family values,
Jane either rebelled or withdrew.
Often going on hunger strikes
as her rancor and resentment grew.

Jane hated the house that she lived in.
She viewed it as *"squalor and mess."*
She fumed that her space was invaded
when her sister destroyed Jane's best dress.

When Jane fell in love with Morton,
her parents did not approve.
"Wed him and you'll be disowned," they said.
"We'll elope," Jane replied, "and we'll move."

Threatened by Jane's ultimatum,
they accepted her choice of a mate.
And seeking Jane's parents' approval,
Morton struggled hard to placate.

Morton came from dysfunction.
His father would gamble and drink,
his sisters were maudlin and gloomy,
his mom's judgment, always on the brink.

As a young man, Morton was athletic.
Conscientious, he learned a good trade.
His character, solidly decent,
Jane knew Morton would come to her aid.

Jane needed a strong man to guide her
and help lift her out of her past.
But Morton was looking for family.
Once married he joined hers, quite fast.

This wasn't at all what Jane hoped for.
She wanted to get far away.
When War broke, Morton was drafted,
Basic Training was held in L.A.

Jane joined Morton for not quite a year.
When his unit was shipped overseas
Jane moved back to the people she knew.
Liberation was only a tease.

After World War II had ended,
Jane and Morton renewed their marriage.
Jane became pregnant quite quickly,
but that ended in a miscarriage.

Despondent, deprived, and discouraged,
Jane gave up, recoiled and cried.
And, to compound her deep sadness,
her mother got cancer and died.

After a long time of brooding,
Jane became pregnant once more.
She stayed in bed the entire nine months.
"She'd have this baby for sure!"

Soon Jane was blessed with a daughter
whom Jane molded to help win her goal.
Looking and acting like a living doll
was her daughter's impossible role.

Then, again, Jane became pregnant.
This time she delivered a son.
In the hospital Jane caught pneumonia
shortly after her birthing was done.

While ill, Jane could not hold her infant.
And visitors weren't permitted.
Postpartum depression took hold of her mind.
At home, Jane was not quite committed.

Now burdened with two needy children
and a husband she had overrated,
nothing her life seemed to offer
made Jane feel she was compensated.

In public, Jane maintained her façade,
but at home her act was outrageous.
Constantly threatening suicide,
Jane never was all that courageous.

Then, surprise! Jane got pregnant again
and blew everything out of proportion.
Overwhelmed and wanting attention,
Jane threatened to have an abortion.

Instead, this son, Jane overindulged.
The older boy, she tolerated.
Jane's daughter, now a big sister,
thought her own value should be inflated.

In response, Jane told her daughter,
"I love all my children the same."
But her daughter was Jane's anger target
when Jane lost a competitive game.

The years flew by. Jane's children grew.
The youngest, an artist, was gay.
The middle son was a musician.
Her daughter, Jane kept on display.

Jane's daughter was much like Jane, at her age.
She yearned to spread her wings and fly.
So when Jane imposed silly ground rules,
her daughter would mostly defy.

Then Jane's daughter met her true love.
Jane disapproved of the match.
Rather than be warm and welcoming,
Jane closed the symbolic door latch.

"You always said that when I met my man
he'd be greeted without your restriction.
Based on the strain your folks put you through,
I thought your words were meant with conviction."

Jane's daughter, outspoken, called Jane on her lies.
"You're a hypocrite and a big fake."
When confronted with the harsh reality,
Jane baked them a tiered wedding cake.

But Jane's bad behavior continued
with relentless critique and abuse.
Her daughter, with husband, fled from the state
without guilt or a verbal excuse.

"She's living the life that I wanted,"
Jane wouldn't dare say out loud.
"I gave her the strength to confront me.
For that, I'm incredibly proud."

Jane's two grown sons also left home
to venture out on their own.
As empty nesters to fend for themselves,
Jane and Morton could not cope alone.

The shock of not having a buffer
hit Jane and Morton with force.
After thirty-two years of indifference,
they actually filed for divorce.

Morton escaped to the suburbs
to be free from reminders of stress.
And Jane moved in with her sister.
The one who destroyed her best dress!

THE FRATERNITY PROPHECY

Locals near the State college
were offered free tuition.
So education was their norm
for dreams to reach fruition.

Randi and her boyfriend Judd
had promised one another
to marry when they finished school.
"If neither found some other."

Then Judd sprang some jarring news,
"I'm not to be tied down.
I've been accepted to a school
in a Northeastern town."

There was no compromising.
Judd's plan was not inclusive.
Randi's heart was broken,
and his sympathy, elusive.

Randi acted out her pain
by sexting with strange guys,
or sleeping with the bad boys
who told captivating lies.

Randi, at an all-time low,
drove herself to despair.
Her form of flagellation
was to replay each nightmare!

Invited by her cousin Lynne,
Randi left her home
to stay with Lynne until she could
control her sex-syndrome.

Lynne was staid and married.
Marc, had loads of charm.
Their goal, was for Randi
to trust her gut alarm.

They inspired Randi
to pick a good profession.
"Stay in school, get your degree.
Don't sink into depression."

Lynne taught oceanography.
Marc mapped out buried treasure.
As professors, college life
was their main social pleasure.

With Marc, a Frat House mentor,
Randi went to his fraternity.
There she heard the Brothers' oath,
"As one, love for eternity!"

She also met a Brother.
Nate was cute and smart.
When Randi and Nate hit it off,
Lynne felt she did her part.

Nate had all good qualities.
He was honest and respectful.
He didn't judge her lurid past
or make her feel regretful.

Not long after, Randi got
her B.A. in Philosophy.
And Nate earned his M.B.A.
in Coding Steganography.

When Randi and Nate married,
they lived right down the street
from Randi's cousins Lynne and Marc.
The four shared the same beat.

They decided not to have children.
As teachers their views were progressive.
"We're always surrounded by questioning minds,
our own would be much too excessive."

New Year's Eve, the two couples
made arrangements to meet and go out.
On their way to the party
the four of them heard a loud shout.

They strained to hear the uproar,
then saw a high-speed chase
coming in their direction.
It looked like a car race.

Then came the warning siren
that got shriller and persistent.
As they veered, Marc's van was hit.
They all died. It was instant.

When the news reached the Frat House
the Brothers spoke their pain
with words of reserved honor —
Their Fraternity refrain.

"Never will we be alone
as part of this Fraternity.
We live our lives with purpose,
As one! Love for Eternity."

SEEK AND YE SHALL FIND

When the earthquake struck in Haiti
Phara's folks fled Port au Prince.
They became U.S. citizens.
They've not been to Haiti since.

For exercise, Phara jogged.
She'd see the same flushed faces
running around the reservoir,
going through their paces.

Jogging made her feel alive.
She would put down her guard
and face up to the problems
that sometimes were too hard.

Phara went to law school
and was hired by a Firm,
with Immigrants as clients.
Bias made Phara squirm.

Phara's job included hours
dispensing social service.
Valued for her expertise,
she comforted the nervous.

Phara shopped and traveled.
She claimed to be content.
"I have the things I need, and want,
and money to pay rent."

But inwardly she hoped to meet
a man with whom to share
her deep-down secret feelings
and know that he would care.

Phara's dating schedule
had been limited at best.
The men whom she'd gone out with,
never passed her test.

She felt she was not critical
with standards much too great,
but these men weren't Haitian,
so she could not relate.

Confident in her fine face,
as well as her good mind,
Phara turned around that saying,
"Seek and ye shall find."

She wanted to be sought out
and adored for all her worth.
Phara wanted a man's love
to move and shake her earth.

"Ideally, he would be creative,
fine-looking and very wise."
To herself, she made a vow
to never compromise.

Day in, day out, were her routines,
every week the same.
Mostly focused on her work,
justice was her aim.

Then at once it hit her.
"This structure is too mundane.
My habits must be broken
before I go insane!"

So Phara ran at night, this time.
Lit up, the path looked new.
Her gloomy mood was lifted
as she saw a different view.

Deep in thought, and mellowed,
after one lap around
her ankle twisted slightly.
Phara fell to the ground.

She wasn't hurt, just startled
by this sudden, silly fall.
Another jogger helped her up.
"My dream man, strong and tall?"

He left her sitting by the side
assured she was okay.
He then went on to do his laps.
There was no need to stay.

The next day Phara overslept
and had no time to run,
but promised herself she would jog
after her work was done.

This was about the hour
that she jogged the night before.
Phara fantasized she'd see
this man again once more.

Sure enough, *dream man* ran by
in the other direction.
Phara caught his eye and smiled.
She wished for a connection.

She guessed he was an artist
and hoped that he was single.
In her mind she thought up ways
that chance might have them mingle.

She figured she could trip again
and this time start to talk.
*"Maybe even tell him that
it hurts too much to walk."*

But Phara didn't want to fib,
she knew it was unwise.
And while she weighed the pros and cons,
she was caught by surprise.

When she turned the corner
of her lengthy fast paced run,
a young man yelling racial slurs
came at her with a gun.

As she screamed, *dream man* appeared
and saved her from great harm.
He knocked the bigot to the ground
and forced him to disarm.

The cops were called. They came, guns drawn
and arrested the street hood.
Dream man ran off quickly,
having done all that he could.

Weeks went by. She missed her runs.
Some clients were deported.
Phara was concerned some cases
would go unreported.

Distraught about these outcomes,
Phara went back to the track.
But as she jogged her way around
she kept on looking back.

Suddenly, *dream man* approached.
He was the right distraction.
He shook Phara off herself
with jolting brute attraction.

His arms reached out to stop her.
He kissed her on her lips
then ran off without looking back
to see her do backflips.

Phara was electrified
by his outrageous act.
"Dream man likes me," she deduced,
and reveled in that fact.

She now knew his procedure.
He jogged this course each night.
Phara was determined to know
if he's *Mister Right*.

The next time that she saw him
she placed into his hand
her card with contact info.
Hardly a reprimand!

Delighted by Phara's response,
he called her for a date.
He feared he was presumptuous.
She didn't hesitate.

They had a lot in common
the two of them discovered.
By the end of dinner
not a thing was left uncovered.

Wilson, too, left Haiti
after the earthquake struck.
His home was lost, but he was safe
and grateful for his luck.

He got his Green Card legally.
His sponsors paid his way.
They showed the U.S. agency
the reason he should stay.

Wilson was an artist.
Not the art that Phara thought.
He did courtroom sketches
after criminals were caught.

The two now jog together,
in the same direction.
With mutual affection
Phara also has protection.

With *dream man* now a real man,
Phara had no doubt,
"that waiting was worthwhile —
and that he had sought her out!"

FINN AND GINGER

Ginger was a model
seen on billboards and TV.
Finn, a trained detective
had an officer's degree.

Finn's background was proud Prussian.
His kinfolk worked the land.
Though living in America,
they kept their German brand.

Ranked high at the academy,
at tracking Finn excelled.
He and his partner found the drugs
stashed where the dealers dwelled.

Thick auburn hair was Ginger's
most appealing Irish trait.
Commercials that she starred in
showed her graceful dancing gait.

Her face appeared on packaging,
food products that were healthy.
Accessories she often wore
were tailored for the wealthy.

Adapted to big city life,
Ginger made her mark.
To keep her shape and coolness
she ran laps around the park.

Finn had just discovered weed
behind the playground's toolshed.
His mind became distracted
when he saw the feisty redhead.

Finn was viewed as handsome,
but he was never vain.
As his partner, Max, once said,
"Finn's a cop that has a brain."

Now near the end of his career
yet age-wise in his prime,
Finn wanted a relationship,
"Why not one that's sublime?"

So Finn approached her slowly.
His head, high in the air
to demonstrate integrity.
She stopped her run, to stare.

He used his magic prowess
to show her he's much more
than just a starstruck officer
who reinforced the law.

He joined her in a lap around.
She quickened up her pace.
Wanting her acceptance,
Finn let Ginger win the race.

He sensed a common interest,
a mutual attraction.
Finn was quite determined
to show her satisfaction.

A side effect of running
is endorphin elation.
But afterwards, Ginger went home!
Finn to the police station.

Finn wished to see Ginger again,
to meet in that same place.
"Maybe we'll run together,
or I'll give her ample space."

But the next night, and the next,
when Ginger didn't show
Finn's imagination strayed.
His angst began to grow.

Riddled with love fantasies
and deviant illusions,
Finn's work began to suffer.
Insight turned to delusions.

Finn had romantic visions
that he captured Ginger's heart.
He pictured their prized offspring,
"They'll be lively, pert, and smart."

Weeks went by as Finn kept watch.
Each night he scoped the park.
Unrelenting white-hot rage
burned from an unreal spark.

His partner, Max, saw Finn's odd mood
but could not read his mind.
So Max covered for Finn's neglect
as Finn lagged far behind.

This night, Ginger had returned.
Her bodyguard saw Finn gawking.
He ordered Finn to stay away
or be locked up for stalking.

Max pulled out his police shield.
"We're working undercover.
So please stand back, give Finn a chance
to see what he'll discover."

Her guard said, "I'm a private eye,
and Ginger is my client.
She's sober, clean, and innocent,
although rarely compliant."

While they exchanged credentials,
Finn leaped to Ginger's side.
Leaving caution to the wind,
all logic, Finn defied.

Minutes later, her guard yelled,
"Help! Ginger, she was raped!"
Max saw Ginger on the ground.
"Where's Finn? Who has escaped?

Perplexed, Max rushed to find him.
"Finn couldn't have gone far."
Then Max heard the screech of brakes.
Finn was run down by a car.

Finn's funeral was solemn.
Max teared up as he read,
"Finn went astray for Ginger,
a certified purebred."

See, Finn was a German Shepherd,
and Ginger an Irish Setter.
Both prize-winning canines.
Their pups could not be better!

LETTING GO OF BAGGAGE

When everything was going well
Rachel was obsessed.
When it was time to celebrate
Rachel felt depressed.

She learned to mask her feelings.
Her act was always calm.
She turned her outrage inward,
doing herself harm.

When young, she saw her mother
turn erratic moods around.
A call or visit from a friend,
she'd suddenly rebound.

This was Rachel's image
of what she thought was normal.
In private she would cry and scream.
In public, she was formal.

Most of the men she dated
took advantage of her smile.
Her willingness to flatter them
was her survival guile.

Chuck, whom she was dating,
she never told him, "NO!"
He still rebuked her, saying,
"You're a *c*-tease, and a *ho*!"

With girlfriends, they would have the lead
in social situations.
When Rachel dared to speak her mind
she faced ramifications.

Everyone who knew her
presumed she would appease.
Even when she sucked up bile,
it was not enough to please.

At her job, one that she liked,
a co-worker was crude.
When Rachel told their manager
he called her "a dumb prude."

Then Rachel went on a blind date.
Charles seemed understanding,
until he grew impatient
and turned to harsh demanding.

"What is my deficiency?
Why do they walk away?
Girlfriends, boyfriends, those at work.
I can't get them to stay!"

Then Rachel met Roberto
before she could destroy
her dignity and passions.
He said, "Stop being coy!"

Roberto was her therapist
who helped improve her life.
His guidance, and her efforts,
taught her how to handle strife.

He saw she was inanimate
but had just what it takes
to rearrange her values.
Not like other fakes.

Her parents were afraid of him.
Her friends despised her change.
No longer would she acquiesce
to all that they'd arrange.

But Rachel was persistent.
She felt he was a match
who helped her see her inner strength.
Rebuild her worth from scratch.

"Your instinct knows when something's wrong,
and who is a mismatch.
By letting go of baggage
you'll make space for the right catch."

This concept was a challenge,
but she followed his advice.
She called out all abusers,
"They will not torment me twice!"

She didn't need to acquiesce.
By bearing loss up front
Rachel walked away before
they pulled another stunt.

Of course, it wasn't easy.
Rachel lost friends and she grieved.
But with her self-esteem intact
her pride had been retrieved.

She learned the strength of saying, "NO"
to reach her long-range goal.
It meant she said "YES" to herself,
realizing self-control.

When Rachel was more confident,
she went on a blind date.
Good timing and great chemistry!
She found her true soulmate.

INNER PEACE … IT ISN'T OUT THERE!

CHAPTER 1

The strong crosswind slammed the heavy outer door shut behind her and the room vibrated. Her prized Seth Thomas pendulum clock bounced off the wall shattering as it hit the parquet tiles.

"Holy Crap! This can't be happening!" Jenna cried out.

June 19, 1978, 4:00 p.m. was Jenna's defining moment. She stared at the broken symbol of time. The room spun. In a wave of dizziness Jenna crumbled to the floor. She sat there, her arms wrapped tightly around her knees and rocked back and forth.

Her mind raced with repetitive thoughts, "Who am I? What does she want from me? Why can't I ever get it right? I'm so darn tired."

Ten minutes later, when Jenna's husband Michael returned from walking their dog, he found her still on the floor. Their dog ran to Jenna and kissed her tear-stained face. Michael ran over and checked for bruises.

"Jenna what happened?" he asked, his voice radiating fear.

"The clock broke," she cried.

"That's why you're on the floor?" Michael asked with an

INNER PEACE ... IT ISN'T OUT THERE!

incredulous shake of his head as he extended his hand for her to grab onto.

She refused it. "I lost my job," she mumbled, and stayed where she was for another twenty minutes, pulling at her hair and babbling about being a phony-fake-fraud-failure.

"Jenna, call Sam. He's a really good therapist. He's helping me get over my stage fright. I'm confident he can help you," Michael softly coaxed.

COMING THIS SUMMER

TRANSITIONS
Women Writers Group of South Beach

A collection of stories, poems and essays about courage, resilience, and transformation.

The culmination of creative ideas from the Women Writers Group of South Beach. Our planet is in constant change and the authors capture how you have to race to catch up with the evolution of time. A thoughtful journey of 15 authors minds explodes in a collection of both stories and poems. You'll laugh, cry and think about your world and personal passage from your today to your tomorrow. Fast paced, constantly changing the writers take you on a ride filled with humor and drama that crisscrosses the gambit of emotions - a crazy roller coaster of experiences. This book follows the success of Miami Off the Page, their first collection.

ABOUT THE AUTHOR

Dena Stewart has had many careers,
committed to each, for some, several years.

New York Teacher, Editor, Corporate Exec.
Although she advanced, pressure made her a wreck.

In each endeavor, fulfillment was fleeting.
She wanted a challenge that wasn't defeating.

Asked, "In what profession would you be content
knowing, most days, that your time was well spent?"

Answer, "To be a painter as my occupation.
To use art for engagement and education."

As a visionary artist, the genre Dena chose,
her work appeared in galleries, art fairs, and museum shows.

One painting went to UNICEF. Her card was a bestseller.
Dubbed "goodwill ambassador," this designation, stellar.

In 1987, when New York was gray and cold,
Dena, and spouse Stewart, moved to South Beach. That was bold.

There, they joined the nightlife and took part in civic action.
They founded a nonprofit to lead group interaction.

They produced a "model" program to address calamities,
said the President's Committee on the Arts & Humanities.

A City High Commission used its power in bestowing
the honor of naming Dena Stewart, "A Woman Worth Knowing."

Dena joined with Stewart for an online video show.
"Alive on South Beach®™" swells her depths, as newer ventures grow.

She heads art workshops, edits film, does art, and also writes.
Dena penned her memoir that revealed her childhood plights.

For Dena Stewart, obstacles force her to reach and rise.
Her eye is on serenity. Inner Peace, the valued prize.

CPSIA information can be obtained
at www.ICGtesting.com
Printed in the USA
LVHW040746120621
689976LV00004B/496